Break My Heart

(A Pine Grove Novel)

Jean C. Joachim

Moonlight Books

A Moonlight Books Novel
Sensual Romance
Bobby Hernandez, Second Base
Bottom of the Ninth series
Copyright © 2017 Jean C. Joachim
ISBN: 978-1-945360-68-8

COVER DESIGN BY DAWNÉ Dominique
Edited by Sherri Good
Proofread by Renee Waring
All cover art and logo copyright © 2017 by Moonlight Books

PUBLISHER
Moonlight Books

Dedication

To my readers, you're the air beneath my wings.

Thank you for your help and support:
David Joachim, Steve Joachim, Larry Joachim, Diane Nelson, Vicki Locey and Kathleen Ball.

MOVIE LOVERS
LOVE'S LAST CHANCE
LOVERS & LIARS
His Leading Lady (Series Starter)
<u>NOW AND FOREVER SERIES</u>
NOW AND FOREVER 1, A LOVE STORY
NOW AND FOREVER 2, THE BOOK OF DANNY
NOW AND FOREVER 3, BLIND LOVE
NOW AND FOREVER 4, THE RENOVATED HEART
NOW AND FOREVER 5, LOVE'S JOURNEY
NOW AND FOREVER, CALLIE'S STORY (prequel)

<u>MOONLIGHT SERIES</u>
SUNNY DAYS, MOONLIT NIGHTS
APRIL'S KISS IN THE MOONLIGHT
UNDER THE MIDNIGHT MOON
MOONLIGHT & ROSES (prequel)
<u>LOST & FOUND SERIES</u>
LOVE, LOST AND FOUND
DANGEROUS LOVE, LOST AND FOUND
<u>NEW YORK NIGHTS NOVELS</u>
THE MARRIAGE LIST
THE LOVE LIST
THE DATING LIST
<u>SHORT STORIES</u>
SWEET LOVE REMEMBERED
TUFFER'S CHRISTMAS WISH
THE HOUSE-SITTER'S CHRISTMAS
THE SECOND PLACE HEART

Chapter One

After his alter ego, Breaker Winslow, died in a fire, Rick Winslow was reborn. Closing his eyes, he could still feel the heat and smell the smoke. Fear spiked through him at the crackle of a fireplace or the aroma of a barbecue. After the total destruction of his tony Manhattan townhouse, Rick fled to the country. Returning to his hometown, he found what he'd been seeking—solitude, in a house on a hundred acres.

He pulled into the driveway of his new home. Standing by his car, he perused the building. Seedy came to mind, along with dilapidated and creepy. Rick Winslow approached the decrepit farmhouse with caution. Fortunately, the place came with enough land to guarantee privacy and eliminate nosy neighbors. The structure was so far below his usual standard of living, he shivered.

The house possessed a brick chimney on the left. First thing he'd do in this old wreck was brick up the fireplace.

Returning to Pine Grove hadn't been a choice. It had been the one place he could hide, avoiding the stares of strangers. He'd live in peace, get a dog, maybe even branch out to chickens, so he could have fresh eggs. His former life was over, his future lay here.

His cousin, Mindy, had found the property. He'd gone to see it that same day and made an offer the next. Much of the land was open field. He'd let that go to seed and return to native forest, like a wall to hide behind.

He pulled a cap out of his back pocket and thrust it low on his forehead, per the doctor's instructions.

"Stay out of the sun. Your face is gonna be sensitive for a while. Maybe forever. Wear sunblock every day and a hat. Stay away from the beach and you'll be fine. The scars'll fade and you'll look okay soon."

Look okay? By whose standards? He'd never look okay again, never be Breaker Winslow, model, actor, heartthrob of a million book covers. When Breaker Winslow pushed past the firemen and rushed up the stairs to the second floor of his townhouse looking for his golden retriever, he had no clue how ferocious the fire had become.

He'd managed to scoop up Ralph, only to be struck by a falling beam on his way to safety. He'd dropped the dog, who had been buried under a huge pile of flaming debris breaking through the ceiling. Knocked unconscious, he had been saved by the fire department. Breaker's face had been scarred beyond more than a patch job could fix. And Ralph had died anyway.

Now he was simply Richard B. Winslow. Yeah, "B" for Breaker. Rick to his childhood friends and family. Not fit to model, Rick had no other profession. Once it hit the news, the paparazzi hounded him. Every effort to hide had failed and it wasn't long before the picture of his hideous face hit the papers.

Deserted by his adoring public, his *friends*, the three women he'd been sleeping with, and even his mother, he had become a recluse. For a year, he hid out in his cousin's house, until his face ceased to be news. The surgery had healed well, but he would never look the same. Sure, he still had the thick mop of brown hair, piercing eyes the color of the Caribbean Sea, and a body sculpted by hours at the gym, but none of that mattered.

He might as well have died in the fire along with Ralph. His life had crumbled like burnt toast. There was nothing left, not even his beloved pooch. After considering suicide, he allowed his dear cousin to talk him into returning to his roots, where he'd be near her and could find peace.

Here he stood with no idea what the next step would be. A sound coming from the long road that abutted his property alerted him. People were coming. He ducked behind a small grove of trees and watched.

A car came up to the edge of his property and stopped. A man got out from behind the wheel. Rick heard a child's voice holler from the backseat.

"Don't! Papa! Don't!"

The man leaned into the car and came out cradling a small dog.

"Sorry, son. We gotta. He needs doctoring and we ain't got the cash."

Rick watched the man put the dog down on the lawn and get back in the car. The voice came from the backseat again, but Rick couldn't distinguish the words.

"He'll be fine here. Someone'll take him in. Hell, son, he's a dog. He can catch mice and eat 'em. He'll be okay." The man got back in the car and slammed the door. He rolled down the window. "Bye, Sparky. You take care now."

A young boy leaned out the back window.

"Sparky!" He reached for the pooch.

The vehicle lurched forward and took off down the road—zero to sixty in ten seconds. The boy continued wailing until the car faded out of sight. The small dog ran after it. Rick set out after him.

After more than a city block, the dog collapsed, panting. As Rick got closer, he could see the little animal was a pug. It lay on its side, chest heaving, tongue lolling. As Rick approached, the dog whirled around. He pushed up on his little legs, then crouched, growling.

Rick stepped back. The dog held his ground, then turned, looking in the direction of a vague, dusty mist, left by the departing vehicle. The pooch twisted his head to keep his eye on the car, or that's the way it looked.

"Sorry, boy. Your number's up. They're gone," Rick said.

The canine glanced back at him, then sank down, his back legs splayed out behind him, his chin on the road.

"Better get your ass up outta there before another one comes along." But Rick knew there might not be any more down that lonesome road for some time.

"Come on. I've got some chicken," he said, motioning toward the dog. The creature pushed up, walked a few feet, circled a few times, and then peed a little lake on Rick's grass. He returned to his former spot, faced the direction his owner had gone, rested his chin on his paws, and didn't budge.

"You can't wait here. Didn't you hear me?"

The dog ignored him.

"They're not coming back for you! They've dumped you! Deserted you! They don't want you!" He yelled. The pug glanced at him, then trained his gaze back on the road.

Tears clouded Rick's eyes. "Stupid mutt. Okay. You're determined to wait. What the fuck? Your funeral." His voice low, his shoulders slumped, he turned and headed for the house. Once he reached the sagging porch, he stopped and looked back. The dog hadn't moved.

"I get it. Nobody's coming back for me either, buddy," he muttered to himself. After one last look at the pug, he opened the door and went inside.

DINNER WAS A ROTISSERIE chicken, potato salad, and cole slaw from the deli. He cut some white meat up and filled a small dish with it. Walking toward the road, he noticed the canine hadn't changed position. This time, the pug didn't growl as he approached, just turned and sniffed. Rick put the bowl down in front of the little beast.

"I tried to tell you. They don't want you. Honestly. I'm telling the truth. They're not coming back. You're homeless now. Just like me. Sort of. Except I have a house. You don't have anything. I know. Not very nice of me to point that out. I just want you to get out of the road."

The dog ate the chicken and wagged his tail for a moment. He sneezed in Rick's direction, then resumed his vigil.

"You're welcome." Rick opened a bottle of water and filled the now-empty dish. The pug eyed him. As soon as Rick stood a safe distance away, the animal lapped up all the liquid. Rick shook his head.

When the sun went down, the air cooled, making good weather for sleeping. He yawned and stretched his arms.

"Good luck not getting run over. Goodnight," Rick said and headed back.

Returning to the house, he trudged up the stairs, peeled off his clothes, and climbed into bed. There were two pillows, sheets, and a thin blanket on the king-sized bed in the big bedroom at the top of the stairs. With no curtains, he could make friends with the moon while he stretched out. A downward glance showed him the little dog remained faithful and hadn't left. Rick closed his eyes and sleep came quickly.

When he rolled over at six, the morning sun poked him in the eye. He washed up and headed for the kitchen. Soon the smell of brewing coffee filled the room. He stood by the window, then rubbed his eyes, not believing what he saw. That damn dog still lay there in the road.

Wearing nothing but jeans, Rick grabbed a bottle of water and the little bowl and strode out to the edge of his property. He jumped a mile as a blast from a huge horn startled him. Turning, he spied a gigantic truck barreling down the road.

"Must have gotten lost," he muttered to himself. "Come on now, doggie. Time to get up." But the animal didn't move. Rick leaned over, yep the eyes were open, it was alive.

"Shoo! Come on. You've got to get outta here. A truck is coming! The fucking thing'll flatten you like a pancake! Get up! Get up, you stupid animal!"

After all his hollering at the dog, nothing happened. Rick made a split-second decision. He scooped the dog up in his arms and fell backwards into the grass on his butt. The little creature squirmed like a greased pig, challenging Rick to hold on to him. Dust and fumes covered them as the vehicle roared past, missing them by no more than two feet, horn blasting.

"Shut the fuck up!" Rick hollered after the gleaming white behemoth belching out black smoke in its wake.

The dog wiggled out of his grasp, moved a few steps away, and sat staring at Rick. Panting, tongue lolling, the pug faced the man.

"I just saved your life. You could be a little grateful!"

Then he poured water into the dish and shoved it closer. The dog lapped it up. Rick sat on the lawn, knees up, elbows resting there, watching his little companion drink. Without warning, the dog ran over, jumped up and licked Rick's face. The man fell back on the grass as the canine covered both sides with saliva. He laughed, though it was weird to have the tongue coating the right side. No one had touched him there since the surgery. The left was all right, smooth and perfect as always.

The pug backed up, sat on his haunches, and barked. Rick pushed to his feet.

"Okay, okay, yeah. I came back for you. You can come in. Come on. I'm hungry. Let's eat."

He made his way across the lawn with the animal trotting along behind him. Rick put on the radio and scrambled up enough eggs for himself and the dog.

"You're going to need a name. Although stupid might fit, the humane society might have something to say about that. Hmm, let me look at you."

The pug's fur was dirty and matted. He was thin, too thin, making his head look big.

"Boy, no one would ever offer you a job modeling, either. Hmm." Rick stroked the uneven stubble on his bad cheek. Finally, his beard was growing in. The doctor said it would come back and it was. Might be spotty, but it would hide some of the scarring and redness.

"You're pretty scruffy. But then, so am I." Rick took a swig of coffee and continued to stare at the creature.

"None of the nice names, like Sparky, fit you. So Scruffy it is."

The dog barked. Rick refilled his water bowl. The pooch had no harness or collar. Rick had no idea if he had had shots either.

"We need to get you to the vet. Need a harness, too. I'll call Mindy." He checked the clock. Only seven. Too early to call his cousin. She was probably banging her new husband about now. He lounged back in his chair as his mind wandered to morning sex. God, he loved morning sex. Waking up to a naked, sexy, willing chick beat a mimosa as the best way to start the day. Didn't look like that would happen again real soon.

Breaker Winslow had slept with too many women to count. They all wanted his body and to claim they'd warmed his bed. Who was he to stand in their way? More than happy to oblige, he'd become adept at the art of lovemaking. The more he loved, the fewer he'd selected. He'd become quite choosy over where he spread his seed.

Now, he'd be lucky to find a hooker who'd agree to screw him without a blindfold. He'd been celibate since the fire. He rubbed his face again, gently. A soft, but insistent whining caught his attention. Scruffy stood at the back door, wiggling his back end.

"Okay. I get it. You need to go out. Come on, I could use the exercise."

He yanked on a ball cap, opened the door, and the two ran and jumped across the backfield.

"MINDY, I'VE GOT A JOB for you."

"I've already got a job. I run the Pine Grove Playhouse, remember?"

"I need help and you're the only one I can call."

"It's time you got out."

"I can't. I'm the Elephant Man. You don't want the right half of my face to scare old ladies and little children, do you?"

"Knock it off, Rick. It's time you were self-sufficient again."

"It's not just about me. I've got a dog."

"A what?"

"A dog. Pug to be exact. Scruffy. And he needs to go to the vet, but I need a harness and leash for him."

"I have a friend who needs work. How about I send her over? She can be your gofer and you can pay her?"

Silence.

"Okay. As long as she won't faint when she sees my face."

"It's not as hideous as you think. It's a couple of scars on the right side, that's all."

"A couple of scars? Think again."

"Your point-of-view is different. You're seeing it as a model. See it as a regular person. That kind of shit happens to people. They get over it and go back to Walmart during peak hours."

"Send the girl. What's her name?"

"Jessica Lennox."

"Fine. Send her."

"How much will you pay?"

"Whatever she wants." He was in no position to haggle over her fee.

"Okay. I'll see if she's interested."

He hung up. After dragging a chair out on the back deck, he and Scruffy sat in the shade. The dog laid his head down on his paws.

"You're going to need a bed, too. Several beds, I think."

Disheartened, he looked around at the sagging porch and recalled the peeling paint on the window frames and in every room. The bathrooms were one step above an outhouse, and the kitchen was a refugee from the 1950s.

He hated waiting, so he made a few calls. Time to make his life in the boondocks more comfortable.

"Carla, darling. It's Breaker. Yes, I'm still alive. I have a little decorating job for you."

"I don't do 'little' jobs, Breaker, darling. You know that."

"It's a small house. Farmhouse. Out in the country."

"Ugh. I hate to leave the city. How big?"

"Three bedrooms, living room, dining room and big kitchen. Oh, and two baths."

"Only two baths? How will you deal?"

"Get off it. It's a quaint old place. Needs a little work..."

"How much work?" He imagined the calculator that was her brain hard at work.

"Okay. A lot of work."

"Darling, I'd love to help, but I've just signed on to do a townhouse in the East 60's for millions. You understand, don't you? I can't be in two places at once."

"I understand completely. Good luck."

He hung up and erased her number from his contact list. "Bitch," he muttered to himself.

He wasn't surprised at her reaction. Since he'd lost everything, he'd discovered his friends had turned their backs on him. Without his prestige and contacts, he no longer commanded their attention. Everyone shunned him as if he had the plague. Frustrated, he pushed to his feet, pacing on the squeaky wood floor.

He went inside and grabbed a pad and pen. Might as well make a list of everything he needed. His new servant girl would have to get it all since he'd not set foot in a store.

The knocker on his front door sounded as he finished the list and his coffee. Unfortunately, with no curtains up yet, he couldn't hide and decide if he wanted to answer or not. He'd have to add those to the list. A pretty, blonde young woman stood outside.

He tilted his head slightly, hiding the right side of his face as he opened the door.

"Jessica Lennox, Mindy Winslow said you had a job?"

"Yes, yes. Come in. Don't mind the house."

He opened the door. She entered, looking around.

"I haven't really moved in yet. I lost all my furniture in a fire, so I'm starting from scratch."

"Do you need help with that?"

"Yes. Let's talk in the kitchen."

Rick led the way. As Jessica approached, Scruffy stiffened and barked. Jessica stopped.

"Don't mind him. He's a visitor. Leaving as soon as I can find him a home."

Rick leaned down and petted the dog. "Back boy. She's a friend."

Jessica took a seat at the table, far from the dog. The pug circled, then lay down on the floor, keeping his eye on the newcomer.

She opened her purse and pulled out a pad and pen. "What do you need done, Mr. Winslow?"

"Please, call me Rick." He sensed heat creeping up his neck as he watched her reaction to viewing his face. She glanced at him, knit her eyebrows, and then opened her notebook. He relaxed, sitting back in his seat. Looked like she wasn't going to lose her lunch or anything. He breathed easier.

"I need to furnish the house. I need groceries. In fact, I need them every week. And I need dog supplies. Can't take him to the vet until I have a harness and leash. Food and water bowls, as well."

"I can do that. But why can't you go to the store yourself?"

"With this face?" he said, then lowered his glance to his hands.

"Oh, okay. I get it. I can do whatever you want. I charge fifteen an hour, including travel time."

"That's no problem. Can you start right away?"

"Sure."

"Let's get the dog taken care of, then we can talk about the house. I have some ideas."

Jessica glanced around. "This old place needs some repairs, too."

"I know. The people who lived here didn't take care of it. It has potential."

"Oh, it does. It does. I love old houses," she said, pushing to her feet and wandering through the kitchen until a low growl from Scruffy stopped her.

"Don't mind him, Miss Lennox, He's not staying."

"Jess," she said, giving the animal a wide berth.

"I think every room needs something besides painting. And there are all those colors to pick."

She licked her lips. "Sounds like a big project."

"I'm sure it'll take months. But when we're done, it'll be a masterpiece."

"My brother, Will, is a carpenter. He can do a lot of the work here."

"Excellent! You're a one-stop place to shop. Here's the list."

Rick gave her the piece of paper and instructions as well as a wad of cash.

"By the way, what do you do?"

"I bake pies and cakes for the café in town and a few other places. And odd jobs, like what I'm doing for you. I help some of the older people here."

"Oh. I see. Kind of an entrepreneur," he said.

"I guess you could call it that. I'll be back with the dog stuff right away, then do the grocery shopping."

"Good. I want to get Scruffy to the vet as soon as possible. Who knows what diseases he could have? Look at him."

He pointed to the thin, grubby creature.

She wrinkled her nose. "Maybe we should add dog shampoo to this list."

He nodded and followed her to the door. After cleaning up breakfast, he sat on the back porch with the last mug of coffee. Scruffy curled up on the floor beside him. He clicked open a pen and opened a notebook. Rick's gaze traveled over his land—grassy knolls, woods, one lone road, no houses in view. He sighed. Complete privacy, just what he needed.

He put pen to paper.

"Time to make a list, Scruffy. Time to get on with my life." He searched his mind for a place to start but came up with nothing. After fifteen minutes, he closed the book and slid the pen into his pocket. He sipped the last of the coffee and looked out toward the trees.

The dog crept closer until he rested his head on Rick's shoe. He reached down and scratched the pug behind the ears, then stroked his back. Feeling fur under his fingers again soothed him. Just like it had with Ralph. Although, being more of a retriever and a hunting breed, Ralph wasn't nearly as cuddly. Still, he was good company, a faithful protector, and companion.

The little canine sneezed, snorted, and sighed before closing his eyes, getting comfortable on Rick's sneaker. The touch of the animal warmed Rick. No one, besides doctors and nurses, had touched him in such a long time. He missed it. Modeling had involved almost constant touching. Fixing a costume, refreshing makeup, styling hair, adjusting a pose, and he'd loved every minute of it.

But now that chapter was closed. He needed to get something else in his life. Something he could do away from people because he'd be damned if he'd put up with sly glances, concerned looks of pity, or averted eyes. He wasn't Quasimodo, though some days it seemed that way. But he was scarred, and it showed.

He rubbed smooth patches on his right cheek. Shit! Damn! The beard had grown in spotty. He'd counted on the facial hair hiding some of his disfigurement, but it looked like it would be another let-down. Fuck. Disappointment had become his middle name.

Chapter Two

Jess returned with a leash, harness, food, bowls, and beds for Scruffy. Rick called his cousin.

"Okay, now we're ready for the vet. Who and where?"

"Hmm. There's a new vet who took over for Doc Blaine, who's recovering from a heart attack. Doctor Henderson's been here about six months. Here's the number." She rattled it off. "Look, I gotta go. Shy is here to go over the set design for Miranda's new play. Call me tonight and we'll catch up. By the way, how did Jess do?"

"She's fine. Out getting groceries now. You can't take Scruffy to the vet?"

"You'll have to face people sooner or later."

"Face? Was that a pun? A joke? In bad taste, Mindy. Talk to you later." He hung up, took a deep breath, and dialed the vet's office. They had a cancellation and the doctor could see him in an hour.

"This is all your fault!" he said, wagging his finger at the pug. The big brown eyes staring at him almost melted his anger. "I'm supposed to be a hermit. I bought this place to stay away from people, not rush out and meet 'em."

The dog barked.

"I know, I know. That's life, right? I'm stuck. Damn it." Rick put the harness on Scruffy and took him for a walk. Then he fastened the pug in the backseat and drove to the vet's. He grimaced, rubbed his rough chin, took a deep breath, and strode up the walk with the canine in tow. When he entered, the nurse sat at the desk, her head down, writing.

"Rick Winslow. I have an appointment?" He turned his good side to her.

"Mr. Winslow? Any relation to Mindy?" The nurse asked, looking up at him.

"My cousin." He tapped his foot and kept from turning toward her.

"Sweet. Dr. Dani will be with you in a minute," she said, pushing away from her desk and heading for the back of the office.

Dr. Danny? What is he, like Dr. Doolittle?

The nurse directed him to an exam room. He kept his bad side to the wall as he shepherded Scruffy into the room. A tempting female rump bent over and clad in jeans grabbed his attention.

"I'll be with you in a minute," a feminine voice said.

Oh shit! Dr. Danny is a girl! I can't face a woman.

"Look, you're busy, we'll come back later."

"Don't be silly," she said straightening up.

She stared at him for a moment before he remembered to turn. She blinked once, glanced at the pug, back at him, and then spoke.

"Don't I know you?"

"I don't think so. You might be wondering about my face. I can explain."

She turned away from him. "Actually, I'm wondering about him," she said, pointing to the dog. She scooped him up and set him on the examining table.

"What happened to him?"

"Scruffy?"

"You call this poor creature 'Scruffy'? Is that a joke?"

"Sort of."

"It's a very bad one. Who has abused this pug, you? This should be reported to the Humane Society."

His eyes widened as he faced her squarely. No way, he couldn't lose Scruffy. He raised his hands. "No, no. Wait a minute. He's not mine."

"Then I can't treat him. Where did you get him?"

"Please give me a minute to explain."

She made a face, narrowed her eyes, and stared at him. Waiting for his explanation, she held and petted the animal.

"Someone drove up to my place and dumped him. Right by the side of the road."

Her frown deepened. "You expect me to believe that?"

"Call my cousin, Mindy. Call Jess Lennox. It's the truth."

"And you're keeping him? For how long?"

Her glance washed over Rick from top to bottom. Her eyes widened. He still dressed the part of an expensive, successful male model: well-tailored shirt, expensive jeans, and perfectly combed hair. He rubbed his face, suddenly aware he stuck out in this laid-back country town. He'd grown up here but had left it behind for the glamour of the big city.

"I don't know. Forever, I guess. Hadn't thought about it."

"I'll take him. I'm sure I can find a good home for him," she said, cocking an eyebrow before turning her back. She transferred Scruffy to one arm as she took out supplies and laid them on the stainless-steel examining table.

Panic captured his breath. He couldn't lose this little critter. In their short time together, he'd become attached. Pain rocketed through him. As quickly as it came, it morphed into anger. He snatched the dog back.

"You've got some fucking nerve! He's mine. I found him. I'm keeping him. We'll find another vet." He headed for the door.

"Hey!" She stood rigid, hands on hips.

Anger flared in his gut. He turned.

"We come to you for help and you try to take the dog away? What the fuck? This little pug has been tossed aside, dumped. I know what he's going through. I brought him to you to save him and this is how you treat me? Like a criminal?" He resumed his path to the door, cursing to himself as tears burned at the back of his eyes. He took a deep breath to steady his emotions. Nope, he surely would not cry because this woman was a bitch.

"No, wait. Wait!"

Rick stopped. "What the fuck do you want?"

"You don't have to get mad. I was only thinking of the animal."

"Were you? You don't want some repulsive man to get his hands on this nice little dog?"

She stepped back. "What? No. I never thought that."

"Then what did you think?" His nostrils flared, adrenaline flowed through his veins. His body prepared to do battle to hang on to his small companion.

"I'm sorry. I just thought. I mean. Well, you *are* Breaker Winslow, aren't you?

"Breaker Winslow is dead." His tone rang harsher than he intended.

"Oh. Guess I made a mistake. Come here. Let me take a look at him." She placed a stethoscope around her neck. You're right, he needs help." Her quiet tone mollified him. She shot a tentative smile his way.

Fear slowly seeped out of his body. "You're not going to take him away again, are you?"

She shook her head. "No, no. I believe you. But this boy is malnourished. He needs medical attention." She wrinkled her nose. "And a bath."

"Okay then. Fix him up." As he handed her the dog, his gaze connected with hers. The frosty blue from a few minutes earlier had softened. He stared at the floor. Pity. He recognized it the second he saw it—pity. He hated it worse than derision. Nobody needed to pity Breaker Winslow. He was a rich son-of-a-bitch. Even if he had lost his profession, his total identity in the fire, at least he had enough money to lick his wounds in high style.

The doctor gave the dog shots, flea and tick protector, eye medicine, and took some blood to run tests.

"I see now what that asshole meant when he said Scruffy was expensive."

"He was probably referring to the eye medicine. He's going to need it for the rest of his life."

"How old is he, doc?"

"Looking at his teeth, I'd say, maybe two?"

"That's good. He'll be around for a long time."

"With proper care, food, and exercise, he should last."

"Good."

"Oh, one more thing," Dani said.

He raised his eyebrows. "What's that?"

"For God's sake, give him a new name!"

Rick cracked up. It was the last thing he expected. "What do you suggest?"

"Anything *but* Scruffy!"

"I'll think about it."

"Once you get him cleaned up, he'll be handsome. Let me do his claws." She plucked a doggie nail clipper out of a drawer. The pug squirmed. Rick placed big hands on either side of the pooch and spoke calmly to him, keeping him still. Dr. Dani stood a few inches away. He smelled lilacs. Must have been her perfume. Damn, the scent caused activity in his groin.

When she finished, she gently placed the dog on the floor.

"That's it. You can pay at the desk."

"Thank you," he said, offering his hand. She shook it with firm confidence. The softness of her skin reminded him of being Breaker Winslow, womanizer. He'd always had women in his life. Touching them, kissing them, making love to them had been his favorite hobbies. It had been so long, he couldn't remember the last time his thumb had raked across a tender hand.

She opened the door, and he took the hint.

"Don't forget. A thorough bath and a new name."

"Got it," he said with a nod. He approached the receptionist. "Miss, can you give me the name of a good dog grooming place?"

She burst out laughing. "It's Nancy. Boy, are you in the wrong town! Everyone here grooms their own dog. Have you got a hose? Nothing more refreshing than a bath out in the backyard with a little shampoo and the hose on a warm day. Groomer. Really? In Pine Grove? You're funny. That'll be two hundred and fifty dollars."

He gave the woman his credit card.

"Oh, here. Eye medicine. Give it to him once a day. I'll give you an extra tube."

Scruffy strained to get out. Rick chuckled to himself. *Smart dog. Already hates the place.* He recalled how his brave retriever had dissolved into a mass of quivering jelly every time he had to go to the vet. Looks like Scruffy followed in his footsteps.

DANI HENDERSON WAITED until Rick cleared the waiting room before she sauntered out. She leaned against the front desk. The receptionist turned to her.

"What planet is that man from?"

"Who?" Dani asked.

"Winslow."

"Why?" Dani shifted her weight.

"He asked me for the nearest groomer." Nancy burst into laughter.

"Really?"

"He must be from Mars. Can you imagine? A groomer in Pine Grove?"

"Nancy, you didn't think he was repulsive, did you?"

"Winslow? Nope. Kinda cute, if you ask me. The scars make him look interesting."

"You didn't recognize him?"

"Should I?"

"He's Breaker Winslow, the model."

"The model?"

Dani nodded.

"Well shear my sheep! Never would have guessed."

"Is that because of his face?"

"Nope. I have no idea who that is. Never seen Breaker Winslow before. Kinda like his name, though."

"He's on a million book covers. Ads in magazines? You've never seen him?"

"Oh, wait. Maybe, that one time I went to Florida to see my folks. I looked at a couple of books in the airport. There was one very handsome guy on a western book. Coulda been him."

"He's hot."

Nancy nodded.

"His accident didn't destroy his looks," Dani said.

"Bet he's not getting many calls from book publishers, though."

"Probably not. I like the way he looks. Kind of gives him character, you know? He's not just another pretty face."

"That he isn't. I agree. He's still pretty good lookin'. Especially around these parts. Not much to look at here, in the way of men."

"There are a few."

"Either married or too young."

"Nancy! What would that cute guy at the feed store say?"

"Cal? He'd just laugh."

"He'd better be careful."

"We're not actually dating or anything. Not yet, anyway."

"Ouch! Get that guy in gear," Dani said, patting her friend's arm.

"He'll come around. He knows I like him, and I'm the loyal type."

"I know you are. And I appreciate that," Dani responded.

"I bet you do. Everyone quitting because they didn't want to work for a woman. Sure left you short-handed."

"Sure did. Who's next?"

"We got a cat to spay due in about ten minutes."

"Good. Time for a cup of tea." Dani headed to the back where the food and beverage supplies were kept.

"Say, you're not sweet on that guy, are you, Doctor Dani?"

"Me? On Breaker Winslow? Nope. Don't think so. He's a pretty angry guy."

"Got good reason, I'd say," Nancy said, as she picked up her pen and wrote notes on Scruffy's chart.

"Agreed." Dani put a mug of water and a tea bag in the microwave.

I suppose he does have reason to be mad. But his face? It's not that bad. And if he turned on a little charm, well he'd be downright dangerous.

She returned to the front desk, sipping her brew.

"'Course, he might do until someone better comes along," Nancy said, carrying on the conversation as if Dani hadn't left the room.

"Doubt I'll have time for any man. There's plenty here to keep me busy."

"Nights here can be long and lonely. 'Specially in the winter."

"Great for sleeping. I'm gonna need rest if I have to get up at daybreak to take care of livestock before the dogs and cats arrive."

"Keep tellin' yourself that. Go ahead. But you ain't foolin' me. That man's looking for something and it seems to me he's found it right here," Nancy said.

"You're mistaken, Nancy. We rescue dogs and cats here, not men." Dani held her cup with both hands.

"I'd say it depends on the man. Some need rescuing real bad, too."

"Maybe, but that's not my problem."

"I say he's gonna be everybody's problem. Somebody better do somethin'."

Dani shot a stern look at her nurse. "Well, don't look at me. I have no room in my life for a man. Any man."

"That's a shame, 'cause that Mr. Winslow, he's something else."

"Yeah, trouble looking for a place to happen."

"If I were twenty years younger and not set on Cal, well..." Nancy's face colored and she didn't finish the sentence.

"You can have him. I have enough to do to keep this practice running. By the way, did we get any résumés today?"

"Nope. Got two yesterday, though. I put them on your desk."

"Thanks. You can change the subject all you want, Doc. Not going to change the situation. That Mr. Winslow? He'll be back. Mark my words."

Before Dani could respond, the front door opened and a man with a carrier entered. A loud yowl emanated from the box.

"That must be our cat now," Dani said, putting down her mug. Relieved to escape Nancy's probing, she went into the back and prepared for surgery.

IN THE CAR, RICK SPOKE to the dog as he maneuvered the vehicle along the winding country road.

"A new name, Scruffy? Let's see. What can we call you?"

The dog barked.

"Poor little abandoned dog? Nope. Too long. Waif? No. Orphan? No. I've got it! How about Oliver? Like Oliver Twist, from Dickens. You know the story, right? Perfect. He was an orphan and so were you. But not anymore. Maybe even Ollie, for short."

Pleased with himself, Rick drove to the house, singing along with the radio. He loved to sing, even though he sang off key. This was the first time he'd raised his voice in song since the fire. He attributed it to the non-judgmental presence of the pooch. Oliver barked his applause when the tune ended.

Upon entering the kitchen, he smiled to see canned and boxed groceries littering his counters and table. Jess had done her job. He opened the fridge. All the perishables rested in their proper places. He rubbed his hands together. Time for lunch.

He rummaged around the boxes and tins until he found the box of dog treats. He'd start training the pug today by teaching him to sit for a treat. Tucked between two cartons of milk lay a deli sandwich. Rick brought it and a beer out to the back porch. Oliver followed along. When he had finished eating, Rick gave the pooch some lessons. Then he unearthed the doggie shampoo from a brown paper bag filled with cleaning supplies. *How appropriate!*

After searching all sides of the house, he came upon a decrepit hose, mended in two places, coiled, and dumped under the porch.

He pulled it out, gently, wiping the cobwebs and dust from his hands on his pants. He screwed it on a rusty spigot in the back and worked the handle hard until it moved. Brown water spurted out in fits and starts.

"The water's rusty, we'll wait," he said. The dog stretched out next to his master. Rick directed the flow away from the pug, not wishing to scare him. He let the dirty water run. There was no nozzle. He grinned, remembering from his youth, how to make water rocket out of a noz-zle-less hose.

Gorgeous from the moment he was born, Rick Winslow had had a fairly normal childhood in Pine Grove until age ten, when his modeling career began. Chief mischief maker on his street, little Rick always had a frog in his pocket and a scheme up his sleeve.

He picked up the hose and squirted the dog. The critter jumped, then tried to bite the stream. Rick aimed again, and the spunky little guy took off, racing around in circles at full speed. Rick ran around and around, trying to wet the dog but failing. Too dizzy to stand, he fell, laughing, onto the grass. Oliver approached cautiously, then licked Rick's face. He grabbed the dog, hugging him to his chest and planting a kiss on his head.

"Dr. Dani's right. You stink, buddy. Come on, let's get you clean."

Rick had never bathed a dog before. The wet animal slipped out of his grasp and kept eluding his master. But the chase continued. Finally,

Oliver ran out of energy and lay panting. Rick snuck up on him, doused him with the hose and applied shampoo.

"This stuff stinks almost worse than you do," he said, lathering up the canine's thigh. When he'd finished covering every inch with suds, he reached for the hose, surreptitiously sneaking it closer. Oliver turned at the sound of the hose sliding along the turf and ran. Rick chased the soaped-up creature as far as the hose would reach. Realizing his master had gone as far as he could, the panting little pug laid down, eyeing Rick, then the hose.

Rick grinned and put his thumb over the end, causing the water to squirt much farther. He managed to douse the dog. When he put it down, Oliver returned, waiting until he stood next to Rick to shake off. Cringing, the man covered his face with his arms as the animal shook and then barked.

There was no getting around it. Between the shower he'd received from Oliver and the crazy hose, Rick was soaked to the skin. He sank down on the ground and called to Ollie, who trotted over. The pug appeared to smile.

"Happy you soaked me, too?" He scratched the furry beast behind the ears.

A bark answered him.

"Come on. Brushing is next," Rick said, pushing to his feet with the pug in tow.

"What the hell?" Mindy Winslow, Rick's cousin, stood by the side of the house, her hands on her hips. "What happened?"

"My first lesson in dog grooming," he said.

"Looks to me like you failed."

"On the contrary. I now have a clean dog, and that earns me an A plus," he replied.

"And a dirty master," she said, laughing.

Chapter Three

The next morning, Jess stopped by to pick up a list of errands. Rick answered the door, in his robe, yawning. Oliver stood with stiff legs and barked.

"Gotta list today?" she asked.

"Nope. You got everything yesterday. Could you stop by this afternoon and give me some ideas about what I should do with this place?"

"Sure. Three okay?"

"Works for me."

He closed the door and made breakfast for himself and the dog. Afterward, he threw on jeans and a shirt and took Oliver outside. Anxious to explore the woods since he moved in, man and pup headed that way.

As a boy, he'd loved the forest. Getting lost in there, discovering new kinds of trees or plants, and finding salamanders and toads had made his day. He'd started a terrarium but had to let all the critters go when he began modeling.

When his time in front of the camera ate up his days, he'd spend any precious spare moments chilling out in the woods. The demanding career had filled his life with people constantly telling him what to do. In the forest, no one pecked at him, no orders, like, "stand up straight" or "stop wiggling" or "don't muss your hair."

He got dirty, climbed trees, let the wind rearrange his locks, and simply led the life of a regular boy. The forest became his haven. The wooded land that now belonged to him beckoned. Exploration awaited.

Much of what he had learned came back to him. A small stream interrupted his path. He stood quietly for a bit, waiting for the familiar croak of leopard frogs. He didn't have to wait long as their mating call reached his ears like a favorite forgotten tune. Oliver spotted something in the water and barked. A big, green, spotted frog leapt out. He hopped along the land with Rick and the dog following.

An old tree, that had fallen some time ago, provided the perfect resting spot. Rick sank down and waited for the pooch to join him. Oliver sat close by and panted. Poking through the thick ceiling of leaves, shafts of sunlight revealed hidden dust particles in the air. Songs of chickadees blended with the *tap-tap-tapping* of woodpeckers.

Rick leaned on his knees and petted his companion as he contemplated what his next steps would be. First things first, as his mother would say. He needed to turn that ramshackle farmhouse into a habitable place. Repairs, painting, sanding, refinishing, he shuddered to think about the size of the job. And then there were furnishings to buy. He only had a bed, a dresser, a chair, and coffee table in the living room, and a small table flanked by two chairs in the kitchen

Did he have anything else to do with his time? Nope. Perhaps fixing up the house was a godsend, allowing him to avoid facing the empty years ahead. Snapping the leash off the harness, he let Ollie loose. The pooch stayed by his side as the two ventured forth, deeper into the brush.

Rick snapped a few photos of graceful trees and beautiful nature designs, then checked his watch—one thirty. They had enough time to get home, eat lunch, and be ready for the appointment with Jess.

As they cleared the forest and hit the field, a car pulled up to the side of the road. It was Doctor Dani.

"How's he doing?" she asked.

Rick picked up his dog and held him to the window.

She sniffed. "He's had a bath. Much improved."

"And he's eating more. I think he's getting over missing his family."

She nodded. "That's good."

"What are you doing here?"

"Back from the post office. I like to take different roads. Get to know Pine Grove a bit."

"You're not from here?" he asked.

"Nope. Rye, in Westchester county."

He nodded. "Nice place. Why'd you come here?"

"For the job. Cool barn. Is it yours?"

"Everything you can see from here, just about, is mine."

"You might fix that barn up. Ever have a horse?"

He laughed. "No. Is that a staple of country life?"

"If you put up a fence, you could keep a horse."

"Wouldn't that be pretty expensive?" he asked.

"Wouldn't a successful ex-model be able to afford it?

Stunned she knew his identity, he had no rejoinder.

"Got to go. Nice chatting. Good job with the dog." She put the car in gear.

"By the way," he said, finding his tongue, "his name's Oliver now."

"Oliver?" she said, raising her eyebrows, directing her glance at the pug. "Suits him. Good choice."

"Thanks."

On cue, Ollie barked, almost slipping from Rick's grasp. Dani hit the gas pedal and the car shot forward, speeding down the lonesome road, kicking up dust in its wake. Rick smiled. He'd actually met a woman who wasn't repulsed by his scars. Well, he hadn't tried to kiss her or anything. Maybe if he did, she'd recoil, but he doubted it.

He thought he knew women well enough to know when one was only being polite and when she was flirting. Dr. Dani wasn't getting a heavy-duty flirt on, but she wasn't exactly putting out "just friends" vibes either. She intrigued him. While he'd stood at her car window, he'd seen inside. Without her bulky white lab coat, he'd noticed a nicely rounded body and some tempting cleavage that started his testosterone flowing.

A quick glance at his watch set him to running. With Jess due soon, he needed to eat before she arrived. Oliver ran along beside him back to the house. A few drops of rain drew his attention. It was late April and the showers weren't over yet. He looked up to see that grayness had set in, covering the early day sun. It was perfect. He could spend the afternoon planning the house renovations, eat, and settle in for the evening with Oliver.

COUNTRY LIVING GREW on Rick. The lack of sirens, honking horns, streets overrun with cars and trucks, and sidewalks stuffed with pedestrians soothed him. Happiness peeked into his days now. Back to his roots? He laughed at the idea. So many years had come and gone since he'd been a country boy. Could one ever go back?

He entered the kitchen at the back of the house in time to hear a knock at the front door.

"Come on in, Jess. Just in time for lunch," Rick said, opening the door.

"Lunch? At three?"

"Does it matter? Are you hungry?"

She grinned. "I could eat."

"Come. Oliver and I are making lunch."

The screen door banged closed behind her as she followed them back to the kitchen.

"You and Oliver?"

"Just a figure of speech."

Rick prepared sandwiches and carried them into the living room. They sat on the floor. He presented a few ideas and she made notes.

"And brick up the fireplace," he said before taking another bite of his ham and cheese.

"What? This beautiful stone fireplace?"

"Yep."

"Why?"

"Don't you read the papers?"

"I know I should, but sometimes I'm too busy."

"Long story short, this..." he said, pointing to the right side of his face, "fire caused this. I lost my entire townhouse, my dog, my career, and my life because of fire. I'll be damned if I'll ever have one, on purpose, in my house."

She placed a hand on his forearm. "Oh my God! I had no idea. I'm so sorry."

"It was a nightmare. And I'm still living it. I don't want to go anywhere near fire of any sort ever again."

"I understand. But let's leave the fireplace alone. You don't have to use it. Put a vase of flowers there. It's decorative and beautiful."

"Not to me."

"There's no way to close it up and make it attractive."

Rick sighed, compressing his lips into a frown. Jess was right. The fireplace had to stay.

"Just because it's here, doesn't mean I have to use it."

"Of course not. Let's go upstairs," she said.

Relieved, he followed her up the steps. The discussion about the fireplace had stirred up unpleasant memories. Even the word fire set his teeth on edge. It had been a more than a year, but it seemed like yesterday to Rick. When he closed his eyes, he could feel the heat, and the panic, the tripling of his pulse, his heart banging against his ribs, and the rush of adrenalin. The smell of the smoke would never leave his nostrils.

Now it made him sick. At the time, it's what saved him from the treacherous third floor. Had he ventured further, he would have died. At least that's what the fire department told him.

Ralph had been up there, barking his head off. When Rick called, the dog ran down the stairs. Smoke thickened rapidly. The dog searched room after room, confused. Rick finally nabbed him, lifting the big canine, and heading for the stairs. Then a beam fell, hitting him squarely in the face, knocking Rick to the floor, and the dog, too. At that point, part of the ceiling collapsed, burying Ralph under burning debris. That's what the firemen had told him. Rick had been out cold. The firemen had carried him out. When they got to the dog, he had already perished.

Even the thought of a backyard barbecue or a gas stove sent shivers through Rick. He'd bought a brand-new electric one for his new home. Although his friends said they understood, he realized that unless they had experienced the same situation, they would never truly feel the fear. He controlled it by talking to himself. Now that he had Oliver, he could chat with the dog and achieve the same goal.

At five, Jess left, vowing to talk to her brother and get back to Rick with estimates on work and a recommendation for an architect. Rick poured a vodka tonic, grabbed a dog treat, and headed for the back porch.

There was a fine line between restful peace and a quiet so still you could lose your mind. Rick bemoaned no gossipy phone calls, no parties to anticipate or dress up for, no photo shoots, no groupies to do his bidding, fussing over him, and admiring him. And no women undressing him with their eyes...and then their hands.

He'd cut a dashing figure in the latest fashions he had received free from the companies he'd modeled for. He didn't know another man who owned three tuxedos. All his clothes had been lost in the fire. Now he owned a few pairs of jeans and the few items that had been out at the dry cleaners when the fire happened. Mindy had teased him about being a fashion plate. Hell, when you looked like Breaker Winslow, you didn't dress in rags.

Being with the right people at the right functions—always a guest at the toniest fundraising galas and private parties—Breaker had grown accustomed to an inordinate amount of attention. After being dropped by every single *friend* and social contact, he'd become a recluse, swearing that was the only life for him. The adjustment to being alone had been almost as painful as gazing in the mirror at the man he had become.

The phone rang, relieving his loneliness. Of course, it was Mindy. Who else would call? None of the three hundred names he'd had in his phone. One-by-one they had disappeared from his life. He'd erased them all after he'd left the hospital. He'd released anger and bitterness with every push of the delete button.

"Mindy, darling. Why don't you come over for a drink?"

"I'm calling to invite you to dinner tonight. Be here at six."

"You assume I have no plans?" he asked.

"Who would you have plans with? You don't know anyone in town except Jess."

"And now Doctor Dani, too."

"Oh? Come for dinner and tell me about it. I've gotta go."

The phone went dead. He frowned then smiled. Now he had a reason to shower and dress up. He'd take Oliver with him.

HE PULLED INTO MINDY and Drew's driveway and parked. He unleashed the dog and strolled up to the building that had been his second home for a year. He'd loved Mindy's house. Old, full of nooks and crannies, but renovated to be comfortable, he'd found it a charming sanctuary. He and Oliver stopped at the door. Mindy yelled, "It's open!"

Man and pug entered. The sound of a loud hiss halted their progress. A gigantic Maine Coon cat stood on the stairs, back arched, fur sticking straight out, making her look twice her normal size. Oliver whimpered and plopped down on the floor.

"It's okay, boy. I'm sure she won't hurt you," Rick said, picking up his dog.

"Don't worry about Minerva. She's all hiss and no bite," Mindy said, kissing Rick on the cheek and shooting a dirty look at the cat.

Once he was unleashed, Oliver took off, nose to the ground, exploring the new territory. Mindy handed Rick a vodka and tonic.

"No, it's not made with fancy vodka. We watch our pennies here," she said, leading him out to the backyard.

Drew manned the barbecue, turning chicken as the others approached. At the sight of the grill, Rick stiffened. Mindy hugged him.

"I'm sorry. I forgot. Do you want to go inside?"

"That's okay," he said, moving a chair far from the flames. "Just don't know why you need an open fire to cook meat when electric stoves are cheap."

Drew raised his palm in greeting, then bent down.

"See this baby? We're prepared for any catastrophe," he said, patting the large fire extinguisher standing next to the barbecue.

Rick downed his drink quickly. Before he could finish another, dinner was ready. Grilled chicken sandwiches with slices of avocado and a fresh green salad graced the table. Oliver whined at the back door until Mindy let him out.

"Is it okay?" Rick asked.

"Of course. Hell, we have deer, foxes, raccoons..." she said.

"And an occasional bear," Drew finished. "Which brings me to this. We have a present for you."

"A gift?"

Drew nodded. "Sorry, it isn't wrapped," he said, putting down his food and rising from the table. He went into the house and came out carrying a rifle.

"Now wait, Drew. Let's not be hasty. I didn't mean it about the grill. Honestly," Rick said, a smile tugging at his lips, his hands raised.

Mindy laughed and Ollie barked. Rick reached down and petted his pooch.

"It's okay, boy. Drew is a friend and he's not going to blow us away with that thing, are you?" Rick raised his gaze.

Drew chuckled, "This is for you, Rick."

"I hate guns."

"You're a city boy. We have lots of wildlife here. Most are okay. But we do have bears. They may come close, looking for food. They may invade your garbage. And, if it's a mother with cubs, look out. They are dangerous. This isn't a high-powered thing. It's just a .22, but it's enough to scare away a bear." Drew handed the weapon to Rick.

He took it, looking it over and holding the site up to his face. The gun was aimed at Mindy.

"No, no!" Drew pushed down the barrel. Don't ever point it at a person."

"You shouldn't give this to me. I don't know how to use it. Sorry, Mindy," Rick said, holding it out to Drew.

"After dinner, I'll give you lessons."

"Drew's right. You need it for protection. You have like no neighbors. Let Drew show you. I'd feel better knowing you have it."

"Okay, okay. Didn't know I was moving to the badlands. I get it. Let me finish this delicious sandwich before it gets cold."

After a dessert of watermelon and blueberries, Drew took Rick out back with the .22, a box of ammo and a couple of tin cans. Oliver trotted along behind. They practiced until the sun went down. Rick thanked them, took the weapon, the ammo, and his dog and drove home.

Rick placed the gun against the wall in the kitchen by the back door. It gave him the creeps. On the way up the stairs to bed, he shared his thoughts.

"Imagine, Ollie, we live in a place that's dangerous enough to need a gun. Wouldn't have helped in the fire though, would it? Could it be that dangerous here?"

The dog gave a yip before he jumped on the bed, circled, and settled down for the night. Rick turned on the bedside lamp, stripped off his clothes, and picked up a book. Maybe a mystery wasn't a good thing to read if you lived in the middle of nowhere. He shook his head to dispel such thoughts and opened to where he had left off the night before.

THE NEXT FEW WEEKS flew by. With help from Jess and her brother, Will, Rick's house renovation project began. Jess carried paint samples back and forth. She took pictures of hardware, sinks, sconces, and other items Rick required to make his house a showplace.

Will started by fixing walls. Next came planing down warped doors so they closed, and updating the ancient bathrooms. Refinishing wood floors and painting walls were last on the list. Rick supervised when needed. When he had to vacate, he and Oliver tramped through the woods or examined the barn and the chicken coop.

When the crew worked at his place, Rick shared dinner with Jess and Will. Rick supplied the food, often pizza, Will's favorite. The model turned up his nose at such fare, bemoaning his fate of having to do without fresh crabmeat, lobster, and prime steak. He noticed Jess and Will laughing at his complaints, so he ceased voicing his opinion, and went along with their wishes, except for buying a barbecue and grilling burgers.

Instead, he bought a grill pan and cooked them on his safe electric stove. New garbage cans were purchased and filled with the debris from his renovation and the leftovers from quickie dinners. Although he didn't tell anyone, he enjoyed the company. Sometimes he'd regale them with stories from his past about glamorous parties, famous people, and celeb-filled outings.

They were an odd pair, a brother and sister so close, yet so quiet. They never talked about their lives, their parents, or their childhood. Rick sensed secrets they wanted left alone, and he respected that. But it didn't keep him from speculating to himself about what they were hiding.

Jess, a pretty young woman with long, light blonde hair and a trim figure, never mentioned dates or a boyfriend. Rick wondered why. A beautiful girl, like her, usually had men drooling all over her. He figured there simply weren't enough eligible men in Pine Grove. She was not his type. He preferred a more mature, confident woman.

It didn't matter who was or wasn't his type. No decent woman would look at him twice, so why even think about it? He put thoughts about finding someone out of his head, relieving himself of having to be social. Hiding out provided the quiet existence he craved.

After a big day and having been up late the night before because he was deeply involved in a suspenseful novel, he got drowsy. The prospect of walking Oliver overwhelmed him. His bed called.

"Tonight, you're on your own, Ollie. Run out there, do your business and come back in, buddy," Rick said, opening the back door.

The pooch stopped at the doorway, looked up at Rick, and cocked his head.

"It's all right. I think you're old enough now to go out there on your own for a few minutes. Just be careful."

The pug sauntered out the door and down the deck stairs to the lawn. Rick eased down onto the sofa and shut his eyes. He hadn't been asleep long before he heard barking. The high pitch hurt his ears. Yawning, he pushed to his feet and made his way to the door.

"Ollie! Stop!" he called as he eased out on the deck. But the barking continued. A growl grabbed his attention. Next, a garbage can sailed through the air, bouncing off the edge of the deck. Still, the pug barked. Rick looked up in time to see a large bear rear up.

"Oliver! Come!" Rick shouted, but the dog paid him no mind. He continued protecting his master and his home. "Oliver! Now!" Rick hollered, backing away from the end of the back deck. The bear advanced.

It leaned down and took one swipe with long, sharp claws at the dog. The powerful creature scooped up the little pug and flung him against the house. The dog squealed. Rick's blood ran cold.

His mind suddenly alert, he ran inside to get his new gun. When he returned, seconds later, the bear had advanced on Ollie. Fumbling with the ammo box, Rick attempted to load the gun. With trembling fingers, he managed to cram three bullets in, cock it and aim. The sound and motion distracted the bear from the injured pup. She turned toward Rick, who raised the gun. His hands were shaking too much to accurately direct the shot. He fired and missed. Taking a deep breath, he took aim more carefully and pulled the trigger. That shot hit the bear, who backed away. Rick discharged the gun one more time, and the bear turned and loped back into the woods.

RICK RAN DOWN THE STEPS to Oliver. Lying still, the pug's breath came in shallow pants. Gingerly, Rick lifted his beloved pet and carried him inside. He yanked his phone out of his back pocket and dialed the vet's office. It went to voicemail.

"Fucking A!"

He put down the phone and plucked a clean dish towel from the cabinet and wrapped it around the bleeding dog. Fear gripped his heart. He couldn't lose Oliver. Nabbing the car keys from the front hall table, he gripped the pug gently, but firmly and headed for his car. It was common knowledge that Dr. Henderson lived behind the clinic. The vet lived close to the office to save time and handle emergencies. Hell, this was a major emergency.

"Come on, buddy. We're gonna get you fixed up. But you gotta hang in there. Don't die, Ollie. Please, don't die."

Rick slammed the car into gear and floored the gas. He had the pug, wrapped in a towel, in the front seat, held by the seatbelt. He roared out of his driveway and down the street.

When he arrived. He threw the car into park, turned the key, and jumped out. He retrieved the injured dog, cradling him in his arms. Not bothering with the front door, which he figured would take her forever to hear, he went around back.

A faint light glowed in a window on one side. *That must be her bedroom. She's still up!*

Hope grew in his heart. He banged on the door. Counted to three, then banged again.

"Coming, coming!"

He paced, hugging the pooch to his chest. She opened the door, tying a sash around her waist.

"This had better be important," she said, covering a yawn with her hand.

Words stuck in his throat. He simply stretched out his arms holding Ollie toward her. "Here. Fix him."

When she saw the whimpering pug, her eyes widened. "What happened?"

"Fix him first."

"I have to know..."

"A bear got him. A bear." Tears forced their way through his defenses. "He was protecting me, the house. And a bear..." but he was crying too hard to talk.

"Follow me," she said, taking the dog and walking through her house. She opened a door that connected to the clinic. Before he could take a breath, they were in an examining room. Doctor Dani disappeared for a moment and returned wearing a white jacket and sweats.

"There's no time to call a nurse. You'll have to help," she said, gathering materials from cabinets and drawers.

Rick wiped his face on his sleeve. "I'm here. Tell me what you want me to do."

As the doctor examined the little fella, Rick stroked his head and spoke softly to him. The deep-voiced sweet words seemed to calm Oliver. Under the doctor's instructions, Rick held the little beast still while she cleaned him up.

"How long before you brought him here? When did you find him?"

"I saw it happen, shot the bear, called you, then drove over."

She glanced up at him. "Shot the bear?"

"Long story."

"Later," she said, returning her attention to Oliver.

Rick held the dog as she shaved his fur and stitched him up.

"He'll have to stay here overnight."

"Then I'm staying, too."

She administered painkiller. "Now he'll sleep. He'll be fine here. Really. Go home. Get some rest."

"No."

She shook her head and rested her hands on her hips. "What do you think you can do?"

"Just be here for him, with him. Whatever. I'm not going home."

"Stubborn ass," she muttered under her breath.

"I heard that."

"I don't care. You're being a stubborn ass."

She eased the sleeping dog gently into a cage and closed the door.

"It's a new place. If he wakes up, he'll be scared. I'm staying. Do you have a blanket?"

"Go ahead. Be a pain in the ass. First, you get me out of bed, then this." She glared at him.

"Ollie got you out of bed."

"He did. You could go quietly. But, no! The great Breaker Winslow has to make a big effing fuss in the middle of the night. Did you see the time? It's almost three."

"So what?"

"So what? I have to be up in four hours. I have a lot of animals to care for tomorrow."

"Shall I relay your message to the bear? Ask him next time to please rip my dog to pieces during office hours?" He shifted his weight. "Rumors to the contrary, I don't have a heart of stone."

She put her hand on his arm. "I'm sorry. I'm just tired."

He patted her hand. "I get it."

When she left the room, Rick slid down, sitting cross-legged in front of the cage. He opened the door and pulled the towel resting on the dog up to cover more of him. It was cool in the room. Dani opened the door and tossed a fleece blanket at him.

"Thanks."

"You're welcome."

"Is he going to be okay?"

"We'll know more in the morning."

"It is morning."

"Shut up. You know what I mean."

"Okay, okay."

"Goodnight," she said, disappearing back to her place. He spread out the blanket and stretched out, content to close his eyes and listen to the pug snore. Soon they were both asleep.

Chapter Four

A shriek awoke Rick with a start. Nancy stood in the examining room. A paper cup of coffee lay on the floor as the contents ran everywhere.

"What are you doing here?"

"Sleeping."

"It's eight o'clock," she said, bending down to retrieve the container.

"Oliver's in there."

"What happened?"

"Encounter with a bear," he said, sitting up, rubbing his scruffy face.

"Last night?"

He nodded and yawned at the same time. Nancy grabbed a handful of paper towels and mopped up the spilled beverage.

"I owe you a coffee."

"I'll take you up on that."

The door opened and a washed, groomed, and white-coated Doctor Dani entered. She slung a stethoscope around her neck.

"Let's take a look at the patient," she said.

"I'll get him." Rick opened the cage and tenderly extricated the dog. A bell tinkled.

"I'd better get going. Looks like the first patient has arrived," Nancy said, leaving the room.

"You're going to look at Oliver first, aren't you?"

"Of course."

She examined the sleepy pug, who yawned, stretched, then shrieked in pain. Rick winced. He held the little critter while Doctor

Dani looked him over. She took his temperature and examined the wounds.

"Nice sewing job, Doc," Rick said.

"Shhh." She listened to the dog's heart. Rick removed his hands and tried to control his breathing. Silently, he prayed for good news.

"He's holding his own, but he needs to stay here. He lost a lot of blood. We need to keep an eye on him for about twenty-four hours."

"Really? He's holding his own?"

"I don't want to take any chances. He stays here. And you don't. Go home. Go to bed."

"I can't stay?"

"I have a practice to run. You'd just be in the way. Be realistic, Rick."

"You're right."

"Besides, you need a shower and some sleep. Looks like we might be calling *you* Scruffy," she said, cracking a smile.

Rick's hand went to his beard, which was longer than usual.

"I'm going. Call me if anything changes?"

"Of course."

He kissed Oliver goodbye and left.

At home, he showered and shaved. He reheated leftover pizza and wolfed it down. Then he grabbed the gun, ammo, and cans. With a bit of trepidation, he peered out the back door. Bright sunshine lit up his property, spreading a sense of innocence and safety.

Nope, no bears—he ventured out. Gun under his arm he trekked to the back by the chicken coop. The remnants of a fence provided the stand he needed. He lined up the cans, moved back, loaded and cocked the gun. He fired and fired and fired until he'd used up all the ammunition.

He'd admitted being afraid of fire, but he'd be damned if he'd let a bear scare the shit out of him, and attack his dog. He needed more ammo. This wasn't going to end until he mastered the rifle and could protect his home, Oliver, and himself. He called Jess and gave her the order to pick up the shells and charge it to him.

His anger melted. He brewed a pot of coffee, but after one cup he dozed on the sofa with his cell tucked under his arm, in case Doctor Dani called. Bending his large frame to accommodate the couch made him restless. Finally dropping into a deep sleep, he had nightmares about bears. Waking in a sweat, he swore to himself that he'd master the gun until he was a crack shot. He'd patrol his property every night until the bears found a new place to roam.

Obviously, no place was safe. A year ago, he'd vowed that fear would never control him. Rick Winslow would do whatever necessary to defend his turf and keep it safe. If that meant having a gun around, then he'd do exactly that. It wasn't just about him, either. He had Oliver to consider.

If you couldn't defend your best friend, what were you worth? Ralph had passed on, but Rick intended to keep Ollie close until a ripe old age.

Within an hour, Jess arrived with the ammo. Rick downed another cup of coffee before heading for the backyard and target practice.

SETTLING IN FOR A BEFORE-dinner snooze, Rick awoke to knocking. It was five, the day was gone. Rubbing his eyes, he stumbled forward, not bothering to look through the peephole. Bears don't ring bells. When the door swung open, his jaw dropped.

"I thought I'd bring him by on my way home." Dani Henderson stood on the front stoop holding a bandaged but fully awake pug.

"Come in, come in," he said, stepping to the side, recovering quickly from the surprise.

She held Oliver in her arms. His middle was bandaged. Rick approached her, arms outstretched. When she transferred the pug, their arms and hands touched. A faint scent of lilacs surrounded her. He towered over her, looking down into lovely eyes. Gratitude washed through him, along with a spark of desire.

"Thank you." He leaned down and kissed her, gently.

She didn't pull away, but her eyes reflected a slight shock. Closing his eyes for a moment, he mentally smacked himself. He took possession of the canine and eased him down on his bed in the living room. He dozed.

"How is he?"

"He's going to be okay. Keep him quiet and bring him in the day after tomorrow. I want to check him out, possibly remove the stitches. Change his bandage twice a day. Give him these antibiotics in his food." She pulled a small plastic bottle out of her pocket.

"Would you like to sit down?" He indicated the only chair in the room.

"No, thanks." She approached Oliver, who lay curled and sleeping. "I brought supplies." She handed him a small bag.

"Thank you again," he said, taking the sack and peeking inside. "Can I offer you a drink?"

Dani took a breath and gazed around the room. "I see you're renovating."

"Yes. I'm afraid the room is not quite fit for company yet. How about that drink? We could have it in the kitchen or out back."

"I'd like to see your kitchen," she said, rising.

"This way," he said, easing Oliver up into his arms and heading toward the back of the house. She followed him. He put the dog in his kitchen bed, then went to the refrigerator.

"I'm going to have a vodka and tonic. Can I offer you one?"

"Please. It's been a long day."

"I bet."

Rick fixed two drinks, added limes, and joined her at the table that faced a large window. She gazed at the panoramic view of the back of his property.

"Must be nice to own so much land."

"Gives me privacy," he said, then raised his glass. "To Oliver's speedy recovery and the doc who saved his life." She clinked hers with his and took a drink.

"Privacy's so important to you?"

"It's everything."

"But your face. It's not as bad as you think."

He laughed. "That's what they call a backhanded compliment."

She gripped his forearm, shooting a tingle straight to his groin. God, it had been a long time since he'd felt the touch of a woman.

"I didn't mean it that way. I think you're overreacting."

"You didn't earn a damn good living from your face, then have it go away."

She let go and gazed at her hand. "No, I didn't."

"Two surgeries and this is the best they could do. To top it off, I don't have one friend left from my life in the City."

He sighed. Giving voice to the truth made it hurt anew.

"I'm so sorry." Her gaze connected with his.

Was that pity or understanding he saw?

"It's over now. I'm here. A new start. And I have Oliver." He glanced down at the sleeping pug.

"I think you're very brave."

He smiled. "I didn't have a choice. My townhouse burned to the ground. I had no place to go."

"You started here from scratch?"

"Mindy's my cousin. She put me up for months until this place came along."

"It's a great house."

"It's getting there. I'm hungry. How about staying for dinner?"

"Well, I didn't have any plans, but I don't want to be a bother." She flushed.

He smiled. Embarrassment was akin to a sexual response—at least Rick believed so, in women, anyway.

"I have to eat. Just as easy to make enough for two." He rose from the table and rummaged through the fridge. "Hmm. Chicken, check. Mushrooms, check. Cream, check." He gathered ingredients on the counter next to the stove.

"Can I help?" She joined him.

"I think there's stuff for salad in the fridge. Could you do that?"

"Absolutely." She opened the door and fished out red leaf lettuce, a jar of artichoke hearts, tomatoes, red onion, and cucumber.

"Let's talk about you," he said, pouring a tablespoon of olive oil in a skillet.

"What do you want to know?"

He turned to her with a grin. "Everything."

She laughed. "Where do I start?"

"How about vet school. Where did you go?"

"Kensington State University."

He nodded. "I did undergrad there. Got to know the dean, Mac Caldwell. Did you know him?"

"I've met him. Nice man."

"He was great, created a special schedule so I could work and still go to school. But this is supposed to be about you. Why vet school?" He cut up chicken breasts and tossed them in the pan.

"I've always loved animals and science. Seemed a no-brainer."

"And was it?"

"I worked my tail off."

"No social life?"

Her cheeks pinked as she wielded the knife, missing the veggie and almost cutting her finger.

"Careful, careful!" he said, taking her hand in his, running his thumb along her palm. "Those are healing hands."

She looked up at him and smiled. He turned away and returned to cutting up mushrooms.

"Uh, social life?" he repeated.

"I had a boyfriend in vet school."

"What happened to him?" He cast a curious glance at her.

"What's it matter?"

"If it doesn't matter, why not tell me?"

She scowled at him and slammed down the knife. "You wanna know? Okay. He was in med school while I was in vet school. We graduated. He left for an internship in Oregon and I went to Philly."

"What happened?"

"Can't you connect the dots? Dean dumped me."

He stopped cutting. "He what? Dumped you? What a fool."

Her face reddened again.

"Any man who let you go is an idiot." Rick turned the chicken. He melted butter in a smaller pan, then added mushrooms.

"You don't know me," she said, adding lettuce to a large bowl.

"I know enough."

They stood quietly attending to their tasks. While the mushrooms and the chicken cooked, Rick pulled down plates. He set them on the table, then stole up behind Dani. He placed his hand on her shoulders and spoke softly, "Did he break your heart?"

She froze as if hit by a blast of subzero air. Her muscles tightened under his touch, and her shoulders rose a little. She nodded. He slid his hands to her arms and whispered, "I'm so sorry."

The words hung in the air like frozen raindrops.

She turned, her body almost touching his. He pulled her into his embrace and lowered his mouth. She wound her arms around his neck and melted against him. The warmth and softness of her body surrounded his heart. His dick woke up. Lack of sex had made his shaft extra sensitive. The pressure from her hips aroused him.

Awareness of what he'd done jolted him. He'd overstepped. With looks like his, he'd only be setting himself up for heartache. Rick stepped back, turning his attention to a pot of rice on the stove.

"I'm sorry. I shouldn't have done that." Now it was his turn to be embarrassed. In the past, a passionate kiss from Breaker Winslow had always met with a green light. But this time—he wasn't sure. Getting turned down would be more than he could handle.

"I'm not," she muttered and turned away.

"You're not?" He took her arm.

"Should I be?"

The smell of burning butter grabbed him. "The mushrooms! Shit!" In three steps, he reached the stove and got to the pan before the contents were burned beyond edible. He turned off the burner and put the pan on the granite counter.

"Got it."

"Why don't you want to kiss me?" She followed him.

"It's not that I don't want to kiss you. Hell, of course I do. But what woman would want to kiss this—?" he said, gesturing to the right side of his face.

"I've got news for you. Scars or no scars, you're still better looking than about ninety percent of the men out there. And looks aren't everything, either," she said, popping a piece of artichoke heart in her mouth.

"That's a funny thing to say to a former model. Looks were more than everything to me. They were the only thing."

She returned to her work at the counter and dumped the rest of the veggies in the salad bowl. "I know. And it's awful. What happened to you, is awful. But your life's not over."

"You're wrong. It is over. That entire existence is gone. Now I, well, I...I don't know who I am." At the stove, he added some cream to the juices in the pan, then sprinkled in flour.

"I guess you have to start over."

"Not easy at thirty-five."

"It sucks. Shit happens. But you'll never get a new life if you hide out here all the time."

"Like you're a big expert? And you have some wild social life here, booked up every Saturday night for months?"

"Maybe I am!" She rested her hands on her hips.

"Are you?" His eyebrows shot up, and his voice squeaked.

"No, but you didn't know that."

He laughed.

"But it's not because I'm hiding out. I just haven't met anyone yet. I'm new here."

"You've been here a year, haven't you?"

"So?"

"That's long enough to find someone to go out with." He drained the rice and pulled utensils from a drawer, then handed them to her. He loaded rice on the plates, topping it with his chicken and mushroom in cream sauce concoction.

"Here," he said, handing them to Dani. After nabbing a bottle of salad dressing, he tucked the salad bowl under his arm and joined her at the table.

DANI PUT A NAPKIN IN her lap and took a deep breath. The food on her plate smelled delicious. Hunger gripped her belly. Rick dug into the meal with obvious appetite. She took a bite and closed her eyes. The chicken was tender, flavorful, and the sauce rich.

"You're a pretty good cook," she said, not wanting to flatter him too much.

"Pretty good?" He sniffed. "You mean, damn good."

"Okay, yeah. I admit it. This is fantastic."

He beamed. "Salad's not bad either."

She shot him a sharp look, and he returned an impish grin. They ate in silence. Images of Rick as Breaker Winslow, stripped to the waist in a fashion ad or on a book cover flashed through her mind. She had been a secret fan of his for several years. She recalled drooling over his book covers in a bookstore or buying a magazine strictly because they carried Breaker Winslow ads for menswear, whiskey, and cologne.

As she sat with the man, a spark of his sexy side emerged. The pictures had shown a lusty man whose appetites could not be contained, a man who took what he wanted. This subdued version intrigued her. Did that other man still exist? Was he real or simply acting?

While he chewed, his gaze connected with hers. A touch of heat rimmed his icy blues. A lopsided grin and an arched eyebrow reminded her of those saucy shots of days gone by. She shivered at the fantasy of Breaker, deciding he wanted her, and removing all obstacles to their union.

"Cold? I can turn on the oven," he asked, rising.

"No, no. Don't bother. I'm fine."

"It does get cool at night. Even in the summer. I remember."

She nodded, wondering how it would be to ward off that chilliness nestled in his arms. *Get your mind out of the gutter, girl.* Her libido wouldn't be shouted down. A glance at his shoulders and chest, so nicely outlined in a T-shirt, reminded her that the rest of him had not been altered by the fire—only one side of his face.

"You okay?" he asked, spearing a piece of lettuce.

Caught staring like a love-sick teen, she sensed her cheeks turning pink.

"Fine, fine." She cleaned her plate. "Let me show you how to change Oliver's bandage, then I must go home." *Get out of here before I do something stupid.*

"Eat and run? Shame on you. One cup of coffee won't hurt, right?"

"Okay."

His smile was warm as he cleared the table. Rick put up a pot of coffee when Dani went to her bag. The two approached the sleeping pooch. Rick knelt down next to her. He proved to be an attentive and capable student. The sleepy dog gave a small yelp, licked Rick's hand, stretched, and then closed his eyes.

"What about food?"

"He'll let you know when he's hungry. Don't wait for a regular meal time. He'll probably wake up some time tonight. Feed him then. Wait until morning to give him more of the antibiotic," she said, standing. The rich aroma of an expensive brew seduced her nose.

Rick stroked the pug one more time, then ambled over to the cabinet.

"I have some biscotti. I don't eat dessert. I don't know why. I won't be modeling again, ever. Old habit, I guess," he said.

She gripped his arm, pulling him down so she could kiss his cheek. His matter-of-fact attitude about the end of his career surprised her. She'd have expected wailing, self-pity, anger, but never cold acceptance. Perhaps everyone dealt with personal tragedy in their own way?

She put her hands on his middle. "Your waist is perfect. Don't mess with perfection."

He laughed, sliding his hands over hers. "Nice to know something on me is still in good shape."

As she wrapped her arms around him, she marveled at the hard muscle beneath his skin. She pressed her palms against his back. She fought the desire to glide her hands down Rick's toned body.

"Nothing wrong with my mouth, either," he said, lowering it to hers.

His lips pressed softly against hers, respectful, too much so for Dani. She pushed her hips flush with his. His soft gasp made her smile.

"Be careful what you wish for," he whispered in her ear. But the pressure against her mouth increased. She parted for him and his tongue explored. Heat grew between them. Dani's legs turned rubbery, and she leaned on him. Rick's hands clasped her hips, holding her to him.

Desire sparked and flooded her body, heading straight to her core. Not happy with abstinence, she melted into him, wanting more. Need rose, goading her, pushing her to make a move. Until common sense intervened.

This man was a customer, a patient. Something, someone who used her services. Should she be panting after him like a dog in heat? *Where's your dignity? Your self-respect?* Gone, like mist in the sunlight.

Rick broke first. His gaze met hers with a questioning look. The flame of embarrassment spread through her face and neck. He'd obviously read her correctly, she'd been ready to give herself to him with one caress.

"Coffee's ready," he said, moving away from her, leaving her skin to cool where he had warmed it.

Of course, he had been right to stop, even though her every gesture had indicated a green light. Why would a man who had made love to models and movie stars want a romance with a frumpy vet anyway? She laughed to herself.

"What's so funny?"

"Nothing."

"Milk? Sugar?"

"Just milk, please."

He nodded, added milk to one mug, and carried the beverages to the table. The gentle snore of the pug grew louder and made Dani giggle.

"Pugs are funny," she said, accepting his offering. "Thank you."

"He's my first pug."

"Did you have dogs before?"

"Just one. Ralph. A golden retriever. He died in the fire." Rick closed both hands around the mug and stared at the liquid.

"I'm so sorry. I didn't know." She squeezed his shoulder.

He smiled and shifted his gaze to hers. "He was an amazing dog."

She nodded and gulped the last of the brew, then checked her watch.

"I'd better be going."

"Of course. It's late."

"I'm inoculating cows tomorrow at seven," she said.

He laughed. "And people think your job is fun and games."

"Hell no! I wear a special suit. Plenty of cow manure to go around," she said.

"Better you than me," he said, taking her mug to the sink.

"Thank you for dinner." She pushed away from the table.

Do I hold out my hand? Can't do that after you've kissed someone, can you?

They strolled to the door together. She reiterated the instructions for Oliver. Rick opened the door. He joined her on the short walk to her car. The moon was only half. The night air had cooled and the sound of crickets accompanied the sweet smell of freshly mowed grass. She took a deep breath. "This air. It never gets old."

"That's one thing I don't miss about the city," he agreed.

"Remember to bring Oliver in for a visit in two days. Call me, if anything goes wrong or you have any questions. Here's my private cell." She scribbled a number on the back of her business card.

"I can't thank you enough."

"It's what I do."

He bent down and kissed her cheek.

"I don't want to...I mean...I shouldn't. Well, you're his doctor and, I mean." He stumbled over his words.

She raised her palm. "I get it. It's okay. Really."

"Take advantage. I don't want to take advantage." He exhaled.

"Oh. Okay." She nodded. "I understand."

"Good. Not that I wouldn't. Maybe I'd better quit while I'm ahead."

Steadying herself by gripping his shoulders, she rose on tiptoe and kissed his lips. "Goodnight," she said, leaving a surprised Rick touching his lower lip.

She slipped into the driver's seat and turned on the ignition. He waved. She pulled out and headed home. That had been a close call. Breaker Winslow was anything but dead, and he'd been weaving his charming web. How inappropriate is it to sleep with a patient's owner? Did that really matter? Or was it simply best to guard her heart against a man with such a widespread reputation as a player? At least those were the rumors, back in the day, when he graced book covers. Maybe she was too chicken to take a chance, risk falling in love, only to lose, again? She didn't have answers, only questions. Time to get some sleep and push all this disturbing desire out of her brain and her body. She had work to do, no time for a relationship, or anything resembling one.

Damn, if she were going to fall off the celibacy wagon, who better to do it with than sexy Breaker Winslow, or his alter ego, Rick? Dani parked the car, fed her two cats, and sat on the bed, staring at the moon. After Dean had broken her heart, she'd opted for the simple life. Spending her days with cows, horses, dogs, and cats was supposed to be easy.

There was no place in her life for Rick Winslow. She sighed. Disappointment lodged in her heart. Could a bit of adventure be a bad idea? She smiled. Perhaps, a short walk on the wild side could be just the ticket?

Chapter Five

Rick tossed, then lay staring at the moon. Sleeping alone had grown old. Sexy Dani Henderson was exactly what he needed. He scoffed to Oliver, snuggled in his bed.

"Are you kidding? What would a smart woman who looks like that want with a disfigured man like me?"

The pug whimpered.

"Really? You think so? Oh, you're uncomfortable. Come on, time to change bandages and give you dinner." Rick threw on boxers and gently picked up the pug. He padded down to the kitchen. The supplies the doctor had left were on the counter. He carried on a running conversation as he changed the dressing. The pug's brown eyes followed his every move.

"Still don't trust me?"

He answered with a low growl.

After he finished and washed up, he set a bowl of wet food on the floor. Ollie sniffed, then wolfed it down. Rick smiled.

"That's more like it."

When he finished. Rick put his rifle under one arm and the dog under the other and went outside.

"Okay, Oliver. Do your business. I'm watching." Rick cocked the gun like an expert and shouldered it, his keen eye perusing the lawn and the woods nearby. He'd be damned if he'd allow a bear to kill his beloved companion.

The words of the therapist he'd seen for six months after the fire came to him.

"When you're ready you'll find someone."

He'd questioned her about any women being interested in a man who looked like him.

"If it's the right woman, it won't matter."

He'd laughed. What a clichéd answer. He didn't believe it for a moment. Fairy tales are fine for books but this was life. His only hope was to find a gold digger who'd put up with his looks and then he'd have to pray the money lasted until he died. The therapist scoffed at him. They'd made a bet that he'd find someone within three years. He'd raised a skeptical eyebrow and offered up a hundred bucks. She'd agreed. That had been his last session.

He stood on the deck, sharp-eyed and ready to do battle. His mind wandered. Could the therapist have been right? Dani didn't seem to mind his face. But then, they were becoming friends, only friends, weren't they?

He smirked. Friends don't kiss like that. How much passion did she have hidden under that prim white coat? Something moved. He heard the leaves rustle. He sprang to attention like a soldier in the field. Now, where was the blasted pug? How could he keep him safe if he didn't know where the creature was?

"Oliver! Oliver! Come, boy. Ollie!"

His eyes searched the area, but he didn't see the dog. Damn it, could the injured pup have wandered away? Rick leapt off the deck in a flash. He called again. This time an answering bark near the woods gave him the dog's location. Rick took off, careful to hold the rifle away from his body.

When he reached the edge. He realized that the rustling was a combination of Oliver and the wind. He picked up the pooch and walked back toward the house. As he eased the dog to his feet, he turned. Something black to the right of where they had just been shifted. It was the bear. It took a step toward Rick, who raised the rifle.

"You fucking monster. Come over here. I dare you. I'll blow your fuckin' head off. Come on, come on, I dare you." His hands trembled as he aimed. The animal stepped back into the shadows and Rick didn't have a clear shot. Instead, he aimed the gun at the sky and let loose.

One, two three, shots. The black bear lumbered into the woods on the other side and disappeared.

"And stay away!" Rick hollered. Oliver barked and barked.

Rick returned. Shaken a bit by his encounter, he eyed the small creature.

"Stay out of the woods, okay?" After stowing the gun, he took the pug in his arms and climbed the stairs slowly, taking care not to jostle his little friend. He placed him at the foot of the bed. Oliver immediately circled before plopping down. Rick could swear he smiled. After pulling down the lightweight blanket and sheet, he shed his boxers and slid in, careful not to disturb the dog, and drifted off to sleep.

TWO DAYS LATER, RICK packed up Oliver in his SUV and drove to Dr. Dani's for the dog's early morning check-up. She unwrapped the bandages, examined the stitches, cleaned him again, and applied fresh covering. She took his vital signs.

"He looks good, Rick. You're taking good care of him."

"Of course, what did you think?"

"You don't have to get snippy. I'm giving you a compliment. Know when to say 'thank you,'" she said, hands on hips.

"Now who's huffy?" He tried to look mad but couldn't and laughed instead. God, she looked beautiful even when she was pissed. "You're right. Thank you."

"That's better. I think we can take the stitches out in three days. Can you come back?"

"I can. But why don't you come to dinner then?"

"Dinner and stitch removal?"

"Why not?"

She smiled. "You're a pretty good cook."

"Good food seduces a woman." He wiggled his eyebrows.

Dani laughed. "At least you're open about it."

"Wednesday?"

She nodded. As he strode toward the door, she stopped him with a hand on his arm.

"Have you decided what to do with that old barn yet?"

"I was thinking of a gym. But there's plenty of room for that in the attic."

"Are there stalls in there?"

He nodded.

"Maybe we could use it to house a homeless horse?"

His eyebrows shot up. "A homeless horse?"

"Sometimes animals in need of rescue come to us."

"Rescue a horse? I can barely handle a dog."

"Just for a few days?"

"Do you have anyone in mind?"

"Ray Watkins is pretty sick. He's eighty-nine. His daughter lives in the City. Ray's got a couple of fine mares."

"And you want to put them in my barn?"

"I don't know. Just thinking ahead."

"Let's talk about it on Wednesday."

"Seven?"

"Works for me," he said heading for the door.

On the short drive home, Rick consulted Oliver. "If we got a horse, he wouldn't sleep inside. You'd still be number one."

The pug barked.

"Okay, I know it's crazy. I don't know shit about horses. But there are books, right? Dani knows everything. She could help me. In fact, I'd put her in charge of the horse. Then she'd have to come over all the time. Maybe even spend the night?"

Oliver woofed.

"You're right. TMI, Ollie."

Rick pulled out his phone and dialed Dani Henderson.

"Okay. We'll clear out the barn and make way for Mr. Ed."

"You will? That's great. I'm sure we can find someone to adopt her," she said.

"Her?"

"A mare."

"Oh. Okay. But you have to help. I don't know anything about horses."

"No problem. When can you be ready?"

"Dunno. I'll start today. Why don't you come over for dinner? You can check on my progress."

"Very clever way to ask for a date. I thought we were doing dinner and stitches on Wednesday."

"It's not dating. It's, it's..."

"It's a date."

"You're still coming Wednesday, right? I guess that's Oliver's date with you. Tonight would be mine. You can tell me what the horse needs."

"Fine. I have late appointments today. I'll be there around eight. Okay?"

"Okay."

He put up a pot of coffee and checked his watch. Only nine, he'd tackle the damn barn after he refreshed with a bit of java. There was a knock on the door.

"Howdy," said Will Lennox. He entered, carrying construction paraphernalia. "Be right back."

He placed a bucket, duffle bag, and paint can down just inside the door. Rick stood back and watched the young man make several trips to his van to schlep in a ladder, step stool, paint pan, brushes, and other tools.

"Major surgery." Rick stroked his chin.

"Might say that. We'll have it done quick."

"We?"

"Yep. I brought my buddy." Will stepped aside to reveal a young, brown-haired man dressed in worker's overalls. "This is Chuck Williams. Chuck, meet the famous Breaker Winslow."

The silent young man stuck out his hand.

"Not Breaker anymore. Just plain old Rick."

"I hope you have somewhere to go because we're going to be working on the first floor and it's best you not be here."

"Suits me. Ollie and I will investigate the barn, then hang out in the kitchen. Is that okay?"

Will nodded as he reached into his back pocket and pulled out a screwdriver.

"If I wanted the barn cleaned out, could you do it?" Rick asked.

"Once we get started, we need to keep going to finish faster."

"Okay, okay. Guess I'll have to do the barn myself." He shrugged and headed for the back door with Oliver tagging along.

He eyed the ancient building with disgust. Red paint had peeled off all but the very top of the building's façade, leaving weathered, gray wood showing. Affectionately called a "neat freak" by his cousin, Rick hated the untidy wreck Dani had referred to as a barn. When they got to the structure, he shuddered as he reached for the big door sporting remnants of chipped and faded red paint. The rusty latch stuck. Rick hit it with his fist, to no avail. Searching the nearby field, he found a rock. Using it, he pounded the pin on the latch until it slid to the side. He opened the door on the right, coughing as soon as the musty, dust-filled air met his lungs.

Particles of dust glittered and danced in the sun, like flakes of gold. Rick swiped at the air, hoping to move it away from him, and stepped inside. Oliver barked and hesitated by the doorway.

"Come on, Ollie. Nothing in here to be afraid of, except maybe a dozen, large rats," Rick said, a shiver shooting up his spine. When the light hit the interior, something flew above his head and out into the open air. Rick ducked and cringed.

"And one medium-sized bat."

The dust in the air didn't dissipate. Rick whipped a handkerchief out of his pocket and held it over his mouth and nose. The interior was in shambles. There were three stalls on one side. Two had rickety doors and one was totally open. The other side had a couple of musty, moldering bales of hay still twined and a ladder.

He looked up. A small loft covered the half without the stalls. He had no idea what was living up there and had no desire to find out.

"Effing city boy," he muttered to himself, shaking his head. In the far corner rested a rusty pitchfork, a shovel, and a broom with bent bristles. Old hay, horse droppings, and more from who-knew-what-kind-of animals littered the cement floor. He picked his way on tiptoe across to the other side.

The floor needed a good sweeping and then the hose. There was no one else around to do it. He grimaced and picked up the broom. Dust clung to the handle. He wiped his hands on his jeans, then grasped the tool again and went to work. Oliver trotted outside, found a grassy spot in the sun, circled it a couple of times, and then laid down. He was snoring before Rick gave three swipes with the broom. Dust and who-knew-what-else flew into the air, clogging his breathing passages. He coughed and hacked until he turned red.

"A trip to Jennings Supply," Rick murmured to himself. He needed goggles and a face mask. "Come on, Ollie," he called, and the dog jumped up and followed him to the car.

Jess had talked about the store. It carried everything from chicken feed to traveling toothbrushes. From listening to her, Rick knew this would be his favorite place. When he pulled into the parking lot, the outdoor section with plants buzzed with gardeners. He ducked his head as he got out of the car with the pug in tow.

He entered the store quickly, found his supplies, paid, and left as fast as possible. He breathed easy when he and Ollie were back in the car heading home. Only one person had stared at him, and it didn't make him want to slug the guy. Maybe he was getting used to his new fate?

When they returned home, Rick donned his protective gear and entered the barn. He'd be damned if dirt, grime, and disgusting things on the floor would defeat him. He picked up the broom. Since he had spent years working out, he was strong. As he swept, Ollie slept. Rick hummed and began to sing a favorite tune, using the sound of the broom as accompaniment.

Raising his voice in song, he moved from the floor to the stalls. He stopped, cracked a bottle of water, and stood back to examine his work. Pleased with the results, the barn looked like it might actually be fit for a horse someday.

A knock startled him. He turned to see Dani leaning against the doorway.

"I'm looking for Rick Winslow. Know where I might find him?" she asked with a twinkle in her eye.

He removed the mask and goggles. "It's me."

"I knew that." She moved closer.

"Got the floor almost done."

"It's lunchtime. I brought you a sandwich," she said, opening a brown paper bag.

"You brought me a sandwich?"

"Yep. My favorite. Ham, lettuce, tomato, mayo, and mustard. One for you and one for me. Can you take a break?"

He wiped his hands on his jeans, which were filthy. "Thanks. Sounds great."

The couple walked into the sunshine. He plopped down on a grassy patch under a tree. She handed him a napkin, and he cleaned his hands again.

"Maybe you'd better use that to touch the food. You're pretty dirty."

Sudden embarrassment washed over him. He'd forgotten what he looked like. *Must be a horrible wreck!* Breaker Winslow, the man with never a hair out of place, always wearing a spanking-clean, perfectly pressed shirt. He must look like an old farmhand or a grizzled cowboy.

"I'm sorry. I wasn't expecting company."

Sitting down across from him, she raised her palm. "I prefer a man who's dirty from work to an every-hair-in-place model." She took a bite of her sandwich.

"Prefer it or not. That's what you got. What's wrong with a clean model?"

She made a face. "A man who's too clean isn't very masculine. Just my opinion."

"Yeah? I know dozens of women who'd disagree," he muttered before bringing the food to his mouth.

"I bet you do. I bet you know thousands."

He finished chewing. "Let's not exaggerate. Not a single one over nine hundred."

She burst out laughing as she fished a bottle of iced tea from her bag and handed it to him.

"You like the rustic, dirt-under-the-fingernails, look, eh?" He grimaced as he examined his.

"I don't mind a little sweat and grime on a man who's spent the day working hard. It's sexy. Love guys who work with their hands," she said, opening the drink.

"I always worked with my hands—and other parts," he chuckled.

She blushed and looked down, smiling. "You know what I mean."

"I can't resist a good setup. You might have a career as a straight man if you wish to give up curing animals."

"Very funny."

"I thought so."

"Just when I'm beginning to think there's a real person under that façade, you do something like this. You're annoying, Mr. Winslow," she retorted, pushing to her feet.

"You're not going?"

"I am. Can't take too much of this sophisticated wit. Poor little country vet like me."

"Now who's being sarcastic?"

"You had it coming." She gathered up the trash and stuffed it in the brown bag.

"Please don't go. I'm sorry. Cut me some slack. I'm new to this life."

"That's true." She appeared to waver.

"Stay. At least until we finish our drinks."

She eased back down on the grass. "Okay. But you'd better behave."

"It's hard for me when there's a beautiful woman nearby."

"There you go again."

"No, really. I mean it." He grabbed her arm, holding her still. "I think you're gorgeous."

"After all those supermodels?"

"They've got nothing on you." His voice softened, and his gaze met hers. She broke the stare and looked down.

"Thanks."

"Don't you know how pretty you are?" His brows knit.

"Dean didn't think so."

"The doctor who moved to Oregon?" He took her hand.

"You're a good listener."

"I always listen to intelligent people."

"He hadn't been out there five minutes before he'd found someone else. I expected him to get settled, then we'd work out how to be together. But I never got the chance."

"He broke your heart."

"I'm over him now. It's been a couple of years."

"Good. Then there is no competition," he said, his thumb stroking the back of her hand.

She withdrew it and returned her gaze to his. "You ruin things for yourself, all by yourself."

"I know. You're not the first person to tell me that."

"Then why do you do it?"

"I don't know. Used to be arrogant. Not anymore." He dropped his gaze to his hands.

"No, you're not."

"Thanks." He looked up.

They sipped their beverages in silence. When they were done, they pushed up and brushed off.

"What do you think of my progress?" he asked, gesturing toward the barn.

"Any horse would be proud to live there," she commented.

"Think so?"

"Especially if she's got no place to go."

They laughed together.

Dani bent to examine the dog. "He's healing nicely."

"Thanks again."

"Now it's time for a check-up. Call for an appointment."

"I will. Gotta wash up. My hands are beginning to itch."

"Allergic to dust?"

"Must be. Thanks for the lunch, the company, and the conversation."

"Any chance you'll have this ready for horses in a couple of weeks?"

"Probably. But only if you help me take care of them."

"It's a deal." She shook his dirty hand then headed for her car. He walked with her. Oliver trotted along behind. He waved as she pulled out of the driveway.

She wasn't afraid to stand up to him. He liked that. Ollie followed him inside. He picked up the pooch and carried him up the stairs, stopping in front of the full-length mirror on the closet door. He gasped.

"Oh my God. What the hell happened to you? Breaker Winslow is surely dead. Dead and gone," he said, perusing his own image. His face was streaked with dirt, dust had turned his hair a shade lighter, and his hands were roughened and filthy.

When Rick headed for the shower, Ollie barked.

"That's right, boy. I'm going to wash off and see if Rick Winslow still exists under this layer of grime. When I'm done, you'll recognize me again."

He stripped off his clothes and dumped them right in the trash can, then slipped under the shower's steaming spray.

AS HE FASTENED A THIRSTY terry robe around his waist, his phone rang. His cousin.

"Are you inviting me to dinner?"

"No. Drew and I are going out. It's date night."

"Oh, damn."

"Sorry. But I am calling with a great opportunity."

He narrowed his eyes. "Why do I think this will involve money from me?"

"Nope. No money."

"What then?"

"Pine Grove is having a carnival day."

"Carnival Day? How quaint."

"Don't be obnoxious. Just listen. It's for charity. We're raising money for the volunteer fire department and ambulance service."

"Don't you pay your firemen?"

"No money."

"Great. So, if I have a fire, and someone doesn't happen to be eating dinner, my house might get saved."

"Don't be ridiculous! Of course, they'd come. They are the best. Anyway, it's a big deal and Jory Walker Stevens, the chair this year, asked me to ask you to volunteer."

"Okay, okay. You convinced me. Put me down for something."

"Don't you want to know what the committees are?"

"No. Just sign me up. Okay?"

"Okay. But you've got to do whatever I sign you up for, deal?"

"Deal. But you owe me a dinner. No, wait. Dinner *and a* pancake breakfast."

"Got it. Have a good night."

She hung up too fast. Rick was suspicious, but what harm could there be in a carnival?

Will called upstairs to say they were calling it a night. Rick pulled on sweats and joined them. They'd be back at eight the next morning. Rick nodded and locked the door behind them. He picked his way around the tools, ladders, and drop cloths to get back to the kitchen. He fed Oliver and heated up a frozen meal for himself.

Shirtless, he took his dinner to the table on the deck. Birds were still at the feeder. Who said he was eating alone? Hell, he had a host of company—goldfinches, woodpeckers, nuthatches, and chickadees all consumed their evening meal with him.

When he finished, he poured a glass of wine and sat in the rocker. Ollie curled up in his deck bed and snored. The evening was so peaceful and the sky so beautiful it took his breath away. Until the peace was interrupted by a phone call. He didn't recognize the number, so he answered.

"Mr. Winslow?"

"Yes. Who's this?"

"Hi, I'm Jory Walker. Actually, Jory Walker Stevens. Newlywed and I forget that's my name now."

"Congratulations," he said. The conversation was already tedious.

"I'm the chair for the Carnival. I'm just calling to say thank you so much. I never thought you'd agree."

"I'm glad to help out. No problem."

"When I asked Mindy what you were best at, she suggested this right away."

Curious as to what his cousin thought his strength was, he had to ask. "Really?"

"Yes." The woman giggled, actually giggled, on the other end of the phone.

Now his curiosity hit an all-time high, and his adrenaline pumped. "Refresh my memory. What did she sign me up for again?"

"How could you forget? The kissing booth!"

He dropped his glass of wine and it shattered on the wood floor.

"Oh my God. Are you okay, Mr. Winslow?"

He could hardly find his voice.

"Mr. Winslow?"

"Rick," he choked out as he bent down to pick up the big pieces of broken glass.

"Okay, I suppose if you're doing the kissing booth, I can call you Rick. I'm going to be the first to buy a ticket."

"I'm flattered." He wondered what she looked like. Then he shook his head. She was a newlywed. "What exactly did my dear cousin say?" An image of her tied to a tree and him with whip in hand came to mind.

"She said that your biggest strength was women, so the kissing booth would be perfect. I'm sure you'll draw a huge crowd."

"The way I look?"

"Don't sell yourself short, Rick. And you'll be in good company."

"Oh?"

"Yes, for the men, my sister Amber, will be kissing, right alongside you."

"Amber?"

"Wait a minute. I'll text you her picture."

Within seconds a photo of the sexiest woman in three counties turned up on his phone.

"Wow. I see what you mean. Do I get to kiss her?"

"You can buy a ticket. But I must warn you, she's happily married."

"Damn. All you great women are."

"We have one in Pine Grove who isn't."

He raised his eyebrows. "Who?"

"Come on, Rick. Everyone knows you two have been spending a lot of time together."

"They do?"

"Doctor Dani. I bet she buys a hundred dollars' worth of tickets. My husband is calling. I've got to go. I just wanted to thank you so much for volunteering. I'm sure we're going to break all the records and raise more money than ever."

"Thank you for your confidence, Jory. Have a good night."

"You, too."

Cursing up a storm, he carted the broken glass into the kitchen.. After clearing away all the tiny shards, he poured another glass of wine. Anger coursed through him.

"Mindy, you conniving bitch!"

Then he put his head in his hands. How could he face women looking the way he did? Jory Walker Stevens was wrong. His booth would be totally empty. Who'd want to kiss a man who looked like him? He blinked away tears, downed the wine, and headed up to bed.

Chapter Six

Rick woke up early the next morning. Panic set in. He had two weeks until the carnival. Maybe he could sell his house and move? The phone rang early. It was Dani.

"Well, well, the kissing fool."

"Oh my God is this all over town already?"

"Of course. It's a small place, Rick."

"I know, I know, but can't a guy have a minute to try and wiggle out of this?"

"Why?"

"With my face, no one will sign up."

"Are you kidding? Jory told me she's already sold fifty tickets."

"Did you buy any?"

There was a moment of silence.

"Yep."

"More than one?"

"Ten."

He laughed. "You can have those for free. Any time."

He heard her embarrassed laugh. "This is for charity." Did she mean that?

"It would be charitable for you to stop by now."

She laughed

"Can't blame me for trying," he said.

"I'll see you Saturday."

"Saturday?"

"You are coming to the chicken barbecue, aren't you? It's the annual one for the firehouse."

"Carnivals, barbecues...for the firehouse? Can't anyone afford to pay for anything in this town?"

"They're fun. Just an excuse to get together. In August, there'll be a pancake breakfast, too."

"Don't tell me. Let me guess. To benefit the firehouse."

She laughed. "Yep."

"Do I have to go to all these things? Can't I just send a check?"

"No! You have to go. Everyone does. People'll wonder why you're not there."

"And I care about that, how?"

"You're living in this town. Don't piss people off unless you need to."

"I need to."

"Stop being a baby. Grow up, Rick. Your pity party, temper tantrum is getting old. Get your butt to the barbecue. I'll be there and so will most of the town."

"If you're going, I'll go."

"You've got to get over this. Get back to life. Most people have crap to deal with in their lives—"

"Not like mine."

"I'll grant you, yours is much bigger. But still, you're alive, healthy, rich—more than most people can say. Make a life for yourself and stop moping. You're wasting time."

He was silent for a moment.

"I'll think about it."

"I'll see you at the barbecue. Gotta go."

She hung up.

Rick filled his mug with fresh coffee and strolled outside on the deck, with Oliver trotting close behind. He grinned as he eased down on the rocker and watched the birds at the feeder. Ollie curled up in his bed and kept an eye on his master.

"Well, Ollie. We're making progress. She wants us to come to the barbecue." He glanced at the dog, who sneezed.

"Oh, wait! She bought ten of those awful kissing booth tickets. Guess she wants me to kiss her. You know, old fellow, I think that can be arranged. And I don't have to wait for the carnival, either." Rick downed the last of his beverage and took the pug on his morning walk.

ON THURSDAY, RICK FASTENED Oliver into the backseat of his car and headed for New York City. He took a room at the tony Savoy arms on Fifth Avenue. He'd returned to check on the rebuilding of his townhouse and visit his surgeon, Dr. Langley. It was a scheduled visit, but he hoped for some good news.

"Rick, you're doing well. This has healed nicely. You might be a candidate for reconstructive surgery."

"You think so?" Hope sprang to life in his chest.

"I do. There's a new procedure being pioneered out in California. I've read up about it but haven't performed it yet."

"Do you want me to be your guinea pig?"

The doctor laughed. "I'm not ready to give it a try on anyone. But I do plan to fly out there and watch for a week or two. There are two doctors heading up the team. Drs. Dean Welling and Mark Joseph. Their schedules are pretty filled, but you're the perfect candidate for them. Besides, with your high profile, their success with you would get national coverage. If you're interested, I'll see if I can get you squeezed in."

"Interested? Where do I sign up?"

"I think you look fine. People don't stare at you on the street, do they?"

"Not anymore." Nope, he lived in a small town where anyone who wanted to stare had already had plenty of chances to get their fill.

"Then why put yourself under the knife, if you don't have to?"

"You don't have my face, my life."

"Do you really miss it that much?"

"Are you kidding?"

"You look good. Healthy. Looks like you've put on a couple of pounds of muscle. Not quite so rail thin. And your color is good, even on your burned side. Country life agrees with you."

"I wouldn't go that far. I'm making the best of a bad situation. You will call them, won't you?"

"I will."

"And let me know?"

Dr. Langley nodded and stood up. After the doctor, Rick headed for his favorite deli where he knocked back a beer and a corned beef sandwich. Next, he ambled over to his property and met with the architect. They were making progress, but he realized it would take at least four more months before the building would be habitable, though far from finished.

On Friday at the end of June, he fastened Oliver into his two-seater and returned to Pine Grove. The air was fresh and the sun hot. He blasted his favorite oldies by ABBA and sang along. Great singing voices didn't run in the Winslow family, and Rick was no exception. What he lacked in tunefulness, he made up for in volume. Belting out songs cheered him as he wound his way up the Palisades Parkway. From time to time, the small dog would howl along with him.

He arrived home as Will and Chuck were finishing up the living room. The paint was still drying when Rick entered. He picked up his pooch.

"Looks great, guys. Great."

"We've got some touch-ups to do. Monday, we'll sand and refinish the floor. It'll look like new."

"Thank you."

Rick gave them a check for their week's work. The kitchen would be next. He could hardly wait. Used to functioning in a gourmet kitchen with professional appliances, he likened his kitchen to cooking out of a chuck wagon in pioneer days.

He put down a bowl of water for the dog, then headed upstairs. To-morrow was that stupid barbecue, and he had to see what clothes he needed. The weatherman predicted the day would be fair, sunny, and on the warm side with no rain.

"T-shirt and shorts weather, Ollie," he said, opening his closet.

He picked out an aqua T-shirt and khaki shorts. The shirt high-lighted the color of his eyes. He'd always been conscious of colors. As a child, he delighted in the colors in his humongous box of crayons. Early in his modeling career, he learned which colors showed him to his best advantage and requested those in wardrobes for jobs for liquor compa-nies and publishers.

He gazed in the mirror and licked his lips. Afraid to believe too much of what Dr. Langley said, he wondered what it would be like if he got his looks back. Yeah, right—when elephants do ballet. Shaking his head, he refused to believe it. He simply couldn't handle more dis-appointment. He changed into work clothes, ready to tackle something he could fix.

"Back to the barn, buddy," he said to the faithful pup at his side. The dog did a half-growl, half-yawn in protest but joined his master anyway. Rick donned the mask and goggles and picked up the broom. He planned to finish today and have the barn horse-worthy within three days.

SATURDAY MORNING, HE went for a run, leaving Oliver home as it was too warm for the short-snouted pup. After breakfast, he picked up a book about the Catskills he'd found at a garage sale. The man who never flinched at paying top dollar for whatever he wanted, surprised himself by catching garage sale fever. The cheap prices astounded him. A dollar still bought something in Pine Grove.

There were things he'd never have considered buying before that seemed to fit his new life. A mirror framed by weathered rope, a country scene painted on wood, a set of rooster and hen salt and pepper shakers, a ceramic teapot with pink and blue flowers. These little things depicting country life charmed him.

When he stopped at these yard events, most people didn't recognize him. They lived in their own little world and top cover models were as far from their lives as Earth was from Mars. He appreciated the anonymity. Being taken as a guy with a few scars on his face, like any man might have who'd collided with the wrong piece of machinery, relaxed him. He'd talked and joked, like any other buyer, with people selling their cast-offs.

Was this the snobby Breaker Winslow? If his fancy city friends could see him, they'd be derisive, make fun of him and his new-found friends and acquaintances. But he had a suspicion that these people wouldn't have turned their backs on him if he'd had the accident here in the country. He suspected they would have shown up with casseroles and helped him rebuild.

He took a long shower, shaved, and slapped on his best aftershave, *La Nuit*. He fed Oliver, then hopped in his car, and headed for the firehouse. He and the pug sniffed the air. They had fired up the grill, and he smelled meat cooking. A few lanterns hung around the huge driveway.

People dressed in shorts, full skirts, or jeans milled around. Will Lennox attended a keg of beer and several containers of sweet tea. His sister, Jess, sat at the money box. Rick stopped and paid.

"Wanna buy a raffle ticket?" she asked.

"Nope. Here. A donation." He handed her a one-hundred-dollar bill.

"Wow! Thank you. That's very generous."

"For the fire department."

"Here's your food ticket. The line forms over there," she said, pointing.

Mike Foster and his wife, Sunny, were standing on a small bandstand while the men tuned their instruments. Rick ambled over, keeping Ollie by his side. Picnic tables were set up on the lawn. Laura Dailey, the woman who baked for the café in town, stood over the food.

"Howdy, Mr. Winslow. Happy you could join us."

"It's Rick, Mrs. Dailey."

"Laura. What would you like?" She gestured to the food line.

There was grilled chicken, slightly burnt and temptingly crispy, corn on the cob, salad, home-made potato salad, macaroni salad, cupcakes, and watermelon. His stomach growled.

"Everything looks good. What did you make?"

"My famous potato salad, of course."

"I'll be sure to get that," Rick said handing his plate to Barney, Laura's husband, who was doling out chicken. When his plate couldn't hold any more food, he picked up plastic utensils and stepped away. Tables filled up fast. Suddenly shy, he didn't spy anyone he knew. Then he heard a voice, a feminine voice, calling his name.

"Rick! Rick! Over here!"

He turned to see Dani waving to him. She was at an empty table, motioning for him to join her. Relief mixed with happiness. He ambled over, keeping Ollie with him. Swinging his long leg over the seat, he eased down next to her.

"Aren't you eating?"

"I finished already. I came early to help set up the lanterns."

"Looks good." He took a bite of chicken.

"How's the barn coming?"

"Almost finished. How about coming over to take a look tonight?"

"Okay. Looks like our horses are going to be ready for new homes sooner than I thought."

"The old man die yet?"

She shook her head. "But he wants to get them cared for before he goes."

Rick nodded.

Dani continued to tell him about the animals while he ate. The food was incomparably good. He hadn't expected any of it to be so tasty.

"Laura Dailey took charge of the cooking, if you're wondering."

"I was."

"She's the best cook for three counties. And she's nice enough to do it for every event."

"The food is great."

"Not exactly the fancy cuisine you're used to."

"It's good. Really good."

Something about this young woman drew him. She was pretty, but certainly not as beautiful as some of the models he'd dated. Still, she had an elusive quality, a warmth...something. He was always at ease in her presence.

People stopped by their table to say hello and chat. From the warmth of the greetings she received, it became obvious that the people of Pine Grove loved Dr. Dani. Pride at being with her swelled his heart.

A few came by to see him. He remembered a couple from a garage sale and the mechanic over the hill, who'd rotated his tires.

Being a famous face, he'd often been recognized on the streets of New York. Sometimes it had been great, but more often it had annoyed him. He'd grown impatient with people taking pictures and gushing. He'd adopted the cynical attitude that they didn't know him and were only impressed by his fame. How ironic then, that when the attention went away, he'd missed it.

Being recognized for being Rick and not Breaker, meant something. The people who greeted him were folks who knew and liked him. Feelings overwhelmed him and shut down his speech. He simply shook their hands, nodded, and smiled when they'd said how glad they were to see him, or they had asked how Ollie was, or if his shooting had improved, and when he'd be by to visit.

A FEW NOTES FROM A guitar drew his attention. Dani was his dance partner of choice.

The first number was a fast one. In the past, he'd have to be juiced to the gills to dance fast at a club. But tonight, he'd try it. If he made a fool of himself, so what? No one would say anything, and he wouldn't find his picture in the local paper. He offered his hand to Dani.

As the light blue sky changed to the deep azure of twilight, the moon made an appearance. A breeze cooled the air as day became night. The lanterns kissed the dancing couples with soft, warm light, and the music turned sweet and slow. Rick took Dani in his arms and led her along to the beat. He'd always had great rhythm and loved to dance.

She softened against him, following his lead. As one dance became two and two became four, he eased her closer, sliding his hands down her back to rest on her waist. She snuggled into his shoulder, her arms circling his neck. Despite their different heights, they were a perfect fit.

The music continued, and Rick lost track of time and place. Only Dani occupied his mind. Her hair smelled of fresh pears. He rested his hand around her neck and stroked the soft skin there. His eyes drifted shut as he leaned his head against hers, and she filled his senses. His body responded as her hips pressed against his. It had been so long since he'd had a woman, but Dani wasn't just any woman.

When the music stopped, he sighed and stepped back. His body cooled at her absence. Her slightly flushed face tilted up. Was that a glow or simply the moonlight? Her eyes were pools of desire. He'd never seen a woman more beautiful. Her fancy T-shirt had a small ruffle along the scooped neck. It tempted him to kiss her and slide the garment down. He needed to stop those thoughts.

Applause snapped him back to reality. The band bowed and packed up.

"Want to see the barn?" he asked, knowing he had more on his mind than that old building.

She laughed. "That's what a country guy says instead of 'do you want to see my etchings?'"

"Seriously. I've got a battery-powered lantern there and a bottle of wine. It's early. No reason to call it a night."

She stepped closer. "I'd love to see the barn and have a glass of wine."

"Good. Get in your car and follow me."

They thanked the organizers. Rick shook hands and a few good ole boys clapped him on the back before he picked up his sleeping dog and headed for his vehicle.

Once home, he ran into the kitchen, grabbed the wine, two glasses, a corkscrew, and a blanket. As he came out the door, Dani drove up. She followed him, along with Oliver, who yawned while he trotted.

Rick took her hand and led her to the old building. He opened the creaky latch.

"Wait here. I'll turn on the lantern."

"You're not afraid of bats?" she asked.

"You had to mention bats, didn't you?" He stopped to glare at her. She chuckled. "I'm not afraid."

"You're a vet. You shouldn't be afraid."

He reached the first stall, where the light rested on a half-wall. After he turned it on, she joined him. He glanced around, awestruck at how the soft light made the dusty old place cozy and inviting.

"This looks great! You've done a wonderful job," Dani said, peering into a stall.

The floor was well swept and hosed down, and most of the cobwebs had been wiped away.

"Thanks."

"The horses are gonna love it in here."

"I was thinking. I should have a bit of a fence built, so they can go outside and walk around a little. Maybe eat some grass? They do eat grass, don't they?"

"They do. Don't go to great expense. They'll probably find new homes quickly."

"Maybe someday I'll have my own horse."

"You?" She laughed. "Not likely."

"You'll teach me how to take care of one, right? I'm doing well with Oliver."

"True. You are."

"Thirsty?" He picked up the wine bottle and tucked it under his arm.

"Sure."

"Come on. There's a perfect spot, right outside."

Rick brought the lantern with them. They walked a little ways away from the barn to a bed of moss. He spread the blanket out and helped her sit. The full moon provided gentle light, but the lantern made it easy for him to uncork the bottle and pour. They toasted to life. Rick leaned back, braced by one arm, and stared at the moon.

"It's beautiful."

She put down her glass and lay back. He stretched out next to her.

"Almost as beautiful as you," he said, leaning in for a kiss.

As he pressed his lips to hers, her sweet scent teased his nose. She tasted like fine burgundy a little sweetened. Any way he sliced it, she was delicious.

Propped up on his elbows, he moved over her. His tongue swiped against the seam of her lips, and she opened for him. He delved in, exploring, his tongue meeting hers. She uttered a soft moan and shifted closer to him. Never one to miss a green light, he pulled her against his chest. She pressed her hips to his.

Feeling her nipples harden, he lost control. He had wanted her, and tonight he'd have her. He raised his hand to her breast. Squeezing the soft flesh brought a moan from her. Ah, no resistance! She was his. He raised his head, licked his lips, and slid his hand under her shirt.

He uttered a silent prayer that he could hold out. It had been so long and his desire was almost overwhelming. A smile graced his lips as he began his seduction.

DANI HAD HOPED THEIR evening would end with lovemaking. She'd stopped by her place to insert her diaphragm, just in case. Though Rick had been a womanizer, it had been two years since he'd been with a woman, or so he said. She prayed that meant he was disease free.

She'd been a fan for a very long time and bought almost every book she could find that had his picture on the cover. Dean used to tease her about it. The first time she saw Rick in person, scars and all, she'd had a physical reaction.

Due to his reputation, she'd expected him to be snotty, selfish, and hostile. She'd feared the man who was so handsome on the outside might be plug ugly on the inside. But the way he'd cared for Oliver gave her renewed hope. Going out of her way to get to know him, the real Rick, had changed her mind. Before she could blink, she'd fallen in love.

Her heart broke for the destruction of his former life. The longer he lived in Pine Grove, the more he seemed to fit in. He'd been in the dilapidated house for only three months, but the man had made friends.

After Dean had destroyed her dreams, she'd tucked her emotions into cold storage. She had a veterinary practice to tend to and no time for foolish crushes. But Rick's heart had touched hers in unexpected ways. She'd found excuse after excuse to stop by his house, or call him. She'd never been an aggressive female. What was it about him that had her out of control? Now in the grip of his embrace, need coiled within her.

There had been no one since Dean. She missed the affection, the closeness, and the sex. She could almost giggle to think what he'd say if he knew who was bringing physical love back into her life.

When Rick's fingers touched her bare flesh, heat flowed through her veins. She practically orgasmed. He kissed like no other. *Wow, this man knows what he is doing.* She shut off her mind and focused on his touch, his kiss, and his masculine scent. Within minutes he had her down to her panties. A shiver of anticipation shot through her as she watched him undress.

The man had an amazing body. She'd seen him shirtless on covers. Once, even a bit of his rear in an ad. And she'd salivated to touch him. She kept hoping to find him without his shirt around his property, but it hadn't happened—until now. He ripped the T-shirt off. The shorts were gone in an instant. Obviously not shy, he shed his boxers next. She feasted her eyes on the body of an Adonis. His shoulders were broad. His chest had just enough dark hair to be enticingly masculine. His pecs didn't rival her breasts, but they were firm. And his abs were defined slightly, but not like a muscle man. His thighs were strong and tapered to perfect calves.

His dick was already erect. She figured he was used to being naked around people. Weren't all models like that? She boldly stared at him and licked her lips. This was going to be an amazing ride.

"Now you." In the light of the lantern, his blue eyes gleamed with lust.

Hesitating for a moment, her shyness stopped her. She swallowed hard. Her body wasn't anywhere near equal to his. Not even on the same planet. But he knew that. She hadn't been a model, just a scientist. He stood, stark naked, holding out his hand to her.

Crickets chirped, breaking the silence of the empty field.

"Have you ever done it outdoors?" he asked her as she pushed to her feet.

She shook her head, sliding her panties down and off.

"I don't think there's a place I haven't done it," he chuckled.

She froze.

He wrapped an arm around her. "This isn't about that. It isn't about the place. It's about you."

"Me?" her voice shook slightly.

"You. Wanting you."

"Me?" she squeaked out.

He laughed "Don't underestimate yourself. You're hot."

She moved into his embrace.

"And sweet, smart, and so damned decent," he whispered.

Tears stung the back of her eyes. She'd missed love more than she had realized. Her body trembled.

"Cold?"

She could only shake her head. He tightened his arms around her, and she closed her eyes, hiding her face in his shoulder—skin to skin. God, it felt good.

"Let me love you, Dani," he whispered.

"Yes," she returned.

Cool air washed over them as he eased her down on the blanket.

"Are you protected?"

"Yes."

He grinned, parking himself between her knees. He stared at her until she worried something was wrong. She knit her brows.

"You're so amazingly beautiful." He opened his fingers and slid his hands down her shoulders, over her chest and belly, to her thighs.

She couldn't rip her gaze from his chest. Sitting up, she flattened her palms against his pecs. A zing shot up her spine as she glided her hands along his muscles. She kissed his chest, then flattened her tongue and sampled his flesh, slightly seasoned with a bit of salt from sweat.

God, he tasted good. He held her head gently and kissed the top again and again.

"Your body's amazing," she said.

He laughed. "A model's product."

"You're in excellent shape."

"Had to be. Never knew when they'd tell me to take my shirt off."

"Did you ever have to take…everything off?" She sensed a blush steal into her cheeks and thanked the shadows.

"Only once in front of the camera. But there were plenty of opportunities to do so after the shoot."

"And did you…"

"Let's not talk about that. I can think of much better things to do than talk." He closed his mouth over hers, then eased her back until she was lying flat. Rick knelt over her, his tongue commanding. She wound her arms around him and let him go to work. Then he added a hand to the mix.

His expert touch aroused her quickly. Curiosity had primed her to respond and made her anticipate their first time. He was more than she expected. His large hand closed over her breast, squeezing gently.

"These are beautiful," he muttered, lowering his lips to taste the willing flesh. She slid her palms up his sides, enjoying the firm muscle underneath. A pinch of her nipple, a lick, a tug traveled directly to her center. Every caress stoked her fire.

"Do it, Rick."

He laughed.

"Really. Come on. I'm ready."

"We've only begun, Doc. And you're far from ready." He slid his hand between her legs.

"You don't think that's ready?"

"Getting there," he began, losing his sentence as his lips glided over her abs and down to her thighs. He clutched the flesh, slipping his fingers north until they came into contact with her core again. He teased her a bit, before parting her legs and diving in. His tongue swept over her nub, sending sparks through her. Her hips bucked up until he steadied her with a firm hand.

"Down, girl." He continued. Passion heated her hotter and hotter. She reached out and grasped a clump of grass and squeezed.

She shut her eyes. "I'm gonna come," she whispered.

He sat up and gently replaced his tongue with a finger inside her, ramping up desire to a thousand. One finger became two. Tension coiled within her. She reached down and closed her hand over his shaft. A soft groan met her ears. She moved her hand up and down.

"No fair," he said, attempting to dislodge her.

"All's fair," she said, tightening her grip some.

"Oh, God, Doc," he said as he fell back and his eyes drifted shut.

"My turn." She scrambled to her knees and thrust her mouth over him before he could pull away. Sure, he could easily overpower her, but when she had him like this, she was in control.

Small moans emanated from him as she went to work. Swirling her tongue around him and bobbing her head, slowly, at first, then faster. After a minute or two, a strong hand grabbed one wrist, then the other one. He broke her hold and pulled her up. His mouth ravished hers. She embraced his shoulders as he secured her waist, gluing her chest to his.

The slight tickle from his chest hair only excited her more. Welded together, he rolled them onto their sides. He flipped her over and mounted her.

"You want me?" He pushed up on his knees.

"God, yes," she breathed.

He shifted her right leg to rest on his shoulder, then rubbed himself against her wetness for a moment before plunging in.

"You got me."

The sound coming from her was a combination groan and gasp. Rick's eyes widened. He stopped.

"You okay, Doc?"

"Hell yes. Don't stop."

He kissed her, then pumped into her. His strokes were easy at first but soon became harder and faster. Dani thought the heat racing through her veins would fry her brain. Overwhelmed by her need for him, she panted as he kissed her neck, then sucked on her skin.

"Hmm, delicious," he muttered.

Desire wound tighter and tighter, coiling like a spring. It started in her loins and traveled throughout her body. Finally, she could stand no more. Her hips bucked up off the ground as everything inside her squeezed. Her breath hitched as a huge orgasm washed over her like a tidal wave. She clutched his shoulders to hold herself steady.

He didn't miss a beat, continuing to pump into her, prolonging her pleasure. Release flooded her veins, traveling all the way from ears to toes. She arched her chest up as he lowered his. Mashed together, she slipped against his sweaty skin, and a sense of calm washed over her.

She turned her attention to Rick.

THOUGH HE HAD NEVER taken drugs, Rick thought this must be what a stupendous high felt like. Every inch of his body had sparked to life. The more he touched Dani, kissed her, loved her, the more intense his feelings. Excitement poured down to his dick, keeping it rock-hard. He pounded away, growing closer to release with every thrust.

It's not like he hadn't experienced sexual highs in his life. He'd had too many to count. But lovemaking with Dani eclipsed them all. He blocked thoughts about love and simply wondered how it could be so different.

He slid his hands around her waist and flipped them over. He wanted to see her, touch her and come, looking at her. Laying back on the blanket, he raised her up and lowered her onto his shaft. She adjusted her legs, riding him like a cowgirl.

He ran his palms up her chest to cradle her breasts before he tweaked her peaks. She moaned with every touch and increased her speed. Her eyes closed, and he'd swear she had had another orgasm. She rode him, squeezing her internal muscles and bringing him closer to ecstasy. He grabbed her hips and thrust her down on him hard, keeping her there, then he could hold out no longer. His balls tightened, and release soared through him like a rocket. He cried out, shutting his eyes, but keeping his hands on her warm skin. He swore he heard birds singing as he came down off his "Dani" high.

Her hand cupped his cheek with a tender touch. He turned his head and brushed his lips against her palm. Emotion bubbled up inside him like a fountain. He tried to quash it, but it was too strong. His eyes watered, but he blinked the tears back. Sure, he'd wanted her body, from the moment he saw her, but tonight he wanted her love, too, and it scared the crap out of him.

She leaned down and placed a gentle kiss on his lips, then her gaze met his. In the moonlight, only the good half of his face showed, boosting his confidence.

"That was life-altering," she said.

Her soft voice floated along the cool breeze to his ears. His heart clenched. His life had been changed enough lately. He didn't need any more, but he couldn't disagree. It had been the same for him, and it would be grubby and dishonest to deny it.

"Me, too."

She dismounted and lay next to him on the blanket. He draped his shirt over her, to protect her against the cool night air. He stared at the sky. The darkness made the ribbon of twinkling stars stand out. He drew her to him, pulling the blanket around them, like a caterpillar's cocoon.

Dani snuggled close, resting her hand and cheek on his chest.

"Nights here are so clear. I never see stars in the City, unless someone hits me," Rick said.

She chuckled.

"It's so peaceful," he muttered.

"That's what I love about the country. There's one time of day when everything stops."

"Nothing ever stops in Manhattan."

"I doubt I'd be happy there."

He hugged her closer. At that moment, Manhattan might as well have been on Jupiter. Country life had settled into his heart. His taste for fancy clothes and cars waned in favor of comfy jeans, flannel shirts, and SUV's. He smiled at the thought he'd ever imagined himself as King of the City a few years ago. The fire had changed more than his face, it had taken away his old life but led him toward a new one.

Was he ready to give up the fame, adoration, and bucks of a top male model? Unsure, he asked her advice.

"The surgeon says there are new procedures. For my face."

"Really?"

He could almost see her eyebrows rise.

"Says it's been long enough. A doctor in California has developed a new way to erase scars. But the guy's schedule is full."

"Plastic surgeon?"

"Yeah."

"What's his name?"

"Dean something. I wrote it down."

"Dean Welling?"

"That's it!" He bolted up. "How did you know?"

"I know him."

"You do?"

"We were engaged. Before he got the offer in California."

"That's your old boyfriend?"

She nodded.

"I hate to ask. You probably despise him. But it would be a huge favor to me if you could help me get in to see him?"

"I can try. He doesn't owe me anything. I doubt he'd listen to me."

His heart beat faster. "I'd appreciate it if you tried."

"Of course. I'll call him tomorrow."

He kissed her. "Thank you."

"What would you do, if you got your face back?"

"I don't know. I like it in Pine Grove. The rebuild of my townhouse in New York is coming along. I could live there sooner than I thought, even though it won't be finished. But I'm not anxious to move back."

"Good." She kissed his shoulder.

"I mean, what would I move back for?"

"I don't know. Seems you have a good life right here."

"Especially with you."

"I didn't want to say that. But I'm glad you did."

"Speaking of you," he said, gliding his hand down her abdomen. "Up for another?"

"Thought you'd never ask."

Rick threw the blanket off and made love to Dani in the light of the moon, and to the accompaniment of the crickets.

Chapter Seven

Dani had declined Rick's invitation to stay the night. Not so much for the gossip that would ensue if someone saw her car parked in his driveway in the morning, not many people drove down that road, but because she needed time to think. She'd promised to call Dean to help Rick get a slot for surgery, but what would that mean for her?

Although she doubted he looked as bad as he thought, he'd been devastated by the loss of his looks, his livelihood, his home, and his beloved dog. Of course, she wanted to help end his agony, but from a selfish viewpoint—how would this affect her? What about their budding relationship? Would a return to gorgeousness destroy what they'd begun building? She'd have to take a chance.

After all, he'd admitted he loved Pine Grove and almost said he loved her. How could she deny him a release from his pain? She couldn't. She couldn't deny him anything. She loved him, and had for several weeks, even if she'd refused to admit it to herself.

Dani climbed into bed and fell asleep within seconds. Nothing like good loving to provide a restful night.

She awoke at six and padded into the kitchen for coffee. She pondered her promise to call Dean. Shaking her head, she couldn't believe she'd agreed to do the one thing she'd hate –talking to Dean, groveling to him for an appointment for Rick. She bit her lip as she poured out the hot brew. Why had she done that? A rueful smile crossed her lips. The crazy things you do for love.

She waited until seven o'clock, California time, to call. Dean was an early riser. Dani scrolled through her phone for his number then dialed.

After a few pleasantries, she got down to business.

"You finally met Breaker Winslow?" The surprise in his voice irritated her.

"Yep. And he's in need of your services."

"Does he know we're booked up?"

"He does. He asked me to intervene. Not that you owe me anything. You certainly don't. But it would be a huge favor if you could squeeze him in."

"Hmm. Breaker Winslow."

There was a moment of silence.

"He might agree to pose for an ad. I mean, he'd be a great before and after shot," she said.

"We can't advertise."

"Then, maybe an interview. Rick, I mean, Breaker, is famous enough to get on national television."

"Good point. Okay. You win. Let me look over the calendar and I'll text you a date. Couldn't deny you anything, Dani."

She rolled her eyes. "Right. But the free publicity won't hurt, will it?"

He chuckled. "You always could call me out, couldn't you?"

"It's just the truth."

"Looks like one hand will be washing the other. I hope he's worth it." She grinned at the note of jealousy in his voice.

"Oh, he is. Believe me."

"I do. I miss you. But I suppose that ship has sailed."

"It has. I'll have Breaker get back to you. Is that okay?"

"Works for me. Thanks for the vote of confidence," he said.

"Always knew you'd be tops in your field. Gotta run. Thank you, Dean. I'm grateful."

She hung up and sighed. That had been easier than she expected. Maybe because her heart was no longer involved.

She headed for the kitchen to put up a pot of coffee when the text came in. The date was six weeks away. Not much time to get her budding love affair with Rick solidified. She'd have to move fast. But first, she had to give him the good news. After adding milk to the brew, she dialed her lover.

"Hey, pretty lady. What's up?"

"Remember that doctor's appointment you were trying to get?"

"You didn't?"

"I did. And you're on the schedule. Let me text you the date."

"You're amazing."

"Just a favor for a friend."

"Friend?"

"Okay, lover?"

"This is wonderful. Thank you from the bottom of my heart."

Warmth spread through her. "You're welcome."

"I love you, Dani. You're, you're beyond words."

"Why don't you come over for coffee? I have a fresh pot."

"Can I bring Ollie?"

"Of course."

"We're on the way."

She hung up and headed for the bathroom. A quick shower would make her ready for another round between the sheets with the world's greatest lover. She couldn't stop grinning as she scrubbed down. Perhaps dreams weren't only for little kids, maybe an adult could have her wish come true, too?

TUESDAY, RICK SPENT the day in the barn. The more he cleaned, the more he found that needed work. A repair here, a replacement there—between trips to the store and buckets of soapy water, he'd been running all day.

As he cleaned, Dani and the impending surgery occupied his mind. A million questions flooded his brain, all involving the woman in his life and what would happen if his face got back to normal? He shoved disturbing thoughts away about the upheaval that might hit him, again, and kept busy. The harder he worked, the less energy he had for thinking. That worked fine.

At the end of the day, he checked the gas gauge to find it flirting with empty. After a trip to the minimart to gas up his car, Rick pulled into the parking lot by the post office. It was eight p.m. Pine Grove had shut down for the night.

He'd gotten out to gaze at the magnificent sunset. He'd never noticed what happened to the sun in Manhattan. He'd always been in the middle of a party or at an intimate dinner with a movie star when the sun was exchanged for the moon.

He eased down on the Viet Nam War Memorial bench down aways from the mailbox to listen to the symphony of the crickets and frogs, as he watched orange streak across the sky and fade into the horizon. A deep teal color arose before his eyes, giving a stunning background for the golden moon.

It was safe to be out in the open in tiny downtown Pine Grove. He didn't have to hide his face or make a run for it. Most of the residents had gotten an eyeful at the chicken barbecue or Jennings Supply. Whoever missed him then had caught a glimpse during his infrequent forays into town. Folks didn't seem to care much about a few facial scars.

He sighed and smiled. Country life had its good points.

"Is that seat taken?" A feminine voice broke his reverie.

Glancing up, he spied Dr. Dani.

"Nope. It's all yours," he said, sliding down to make room.

She sniffed wiping her nose with a crumpled tissue. Her shoulders slumped.

"Tough day?"

She nodded.

"Want to talk about it?"

She shook her head. He shifted around to face her.

"Someone die?"

"A puppy. Poisoned by accident in a careless home."

"I'm sorry." He touched her arm.

"Doc Gregory at vet school told me I'd get used to it, after a while. That's hard to believe."

The dim light from the street lamp reflected off a tear on her cheek. She swiped at it.

He slid his arm around her shoulders and pulled her to him. "What are you doing out here, alone, in the dark?"

"Walking it off."

He held her close and kissed the top of her head.

"And you?" she asked, not moving from his embrace.

"Enjoying the sunset and the quiet."

"Reformed city boy?"

"Perhaps. There never seemed to be time to notice this stuff in Manhattan."

Was he turning country? Ridiculous! Breaker Winslow, debonair, sophisticated, rich, would always crave the heartbeat of the city, wouldn't he? At that moment, the cool fresh country air filling his lungs and the beautiful woman filling his arms represented happiness itself.

"Are you planning to stay in Pine Grove?" she asked through her sniffles.

"I was."

"Was? Does this have anything to do with the new surgery?"

"One thing the fire taught me. Don't make too many plans. Things change. Shit happens, stuff you can't predict. Might even destroy your plans, your dreams, maybe even you."

"But you're not destroyed. You've moved to a different place, made friends, and started a new life."

"Friends? I'm not sure I know the meaning of the word, anymore. I thought I had a ton of friends in the City. But after the accident, it turned out my *friends* were just an illusion. I don't know who to trust, so I trust no one. Much safer that way. Sure, people are pleasant. Give you a friendly greeting. It doesn't mean crap. If I had another fire, who'd come to help me? No one."

"Do you really feel that way?"

"I'm a realist. Ollie is my best friend and only because I feed him."

"What about me?"

"You're my lover. It's not the same."

"Oh no? I'm not your friend, too?"

"Are you?" He leaned back into the light from the streetlamp and cocked an eyebrow.

"Of course, I'm your friend. And, yes, I'd help you if you had a fire. I'd move you into my house, I'd take care of your injuries..." Emotion choked her.

"You would?"

"Don't be an idiot. Of course."

"I knew there was a reason I loved you."

She froze. Had he said the wrong thing, revealed too much? Feelings, friendship, love were new to Rick. He didn't quite know what to say or do.

"You love me?"

Trapped, he had to tell the truth. "I do."

"I love you, too."

"You do?" His voice rose an entire octave.

She laughed. "You didn't know? Didn't you guess?"

He shook his head.

"Why don't you come spend the night with me?"

"Ollie, too?"

"Of course."

"I'll go get him and meet you at your place."

"Sounds like a plan."

He kissed her quickly, then jumped into his car. Pressing the gas pedal a little closer to the floor, he was home in minutes. He dressed Oliver in his harness and leash and led him to the car.

He opened the windows wide and took a deep breath. Fresh country air had seduced more than his lungs. He watched for the gleam of animal eyes in his headlights. The dark of night emboldened the deer, so he needed to be careful.

He parked behind the clinic and released Ollie from the backseat. Before he could exhale, he strode up the steps to Dani's front door. He knocked with his heart in his mouth, his expectations high, and his pulse out of control. Rick readied himself for that roller coaster ride called love.

HE AWOKE TO A LOVELY day. The day Rick dreaded had arrived all too soon. Not the surgery, the carnival! The kissing booth had preyed on his mind for a week. He'd been flossing every night, hoping his breath would be fresh enough. He'd avoided thinking about the women who'd bought tickets. Some would be attractive and kissing them would be a breeze.

But what about the ones who weren't? How would he handle them? God forbid he made someone feel bad. In the old days, he wouldn't have given a damn. But then again, he'd never have agreed to do the booth. Now he had tuned into feelings in a new way. He'd be devastated if he inflicted emotional pain on anyone.

Unselfish feelings were new to Rick. He'd have to figure out how to fake enthusiasm with unattractive women. He'd been talking to himself about it for days. How it was just one kiss and he'd acted in a few movies, so wasn't that the same thing? Couldn't he pretend the woman he had to kiss was Miss America? But the truth about his acting skills won out. He simply wasn't that good.

And what if it wasn't only one kiss? What if an ugly woman had bought twenty-five tickets? He'd pass out, that's all. Holler, "Call 911" and keel over in a dead faint. That was his fall back escape plan, and it gave him some peace. At least the booth was only open at eleven. He had sworn a dozen times he'd get back at Mindy for signing him up.

The sun was out and a breeze cooled his deck. After walking Oliver, he and the pooch settled down there, Rick with his coffee and Ollie curled up in his bed. He frowned to see his prayers for a sudden tornado or hurricane had not been answered. Only torrential rain could save him from a fate worse thaan death—kissing strange women.

And what if they didn't know about his accident and were horrified and repulsed when they saw him in the flesh. He shuddered. He'd quit. He'd just walk away. Too bad for the fire department, he could only take so much humiliation.

He scowled at the sun and retrieved the newspaper from his front porch. Rifling through to get to the weather report, his dismay grew when he read, *sunny, high of eighty, zero chance of rain.* How he'd wished bad weather would cancel the carnival. Then he could take all the kudos for having volunteered without the degradation of having to follow through.

Heading for the kitchen, he decided to drown his sorrows in a sour cream and caviar omelet plus a mimosa. Hell, he'd simply stuff a straw into the champagne bottle and drink his fill. Why get a clean flute dirty? Maybe doing the kissing booth drunk would be easier? Maybe the women would flee when they smelled alcohol on him. A devilish grin raised his lips.

As the omelet simmered on the stove, the doorbell rang.

"Rick!" It was Mindy.

"Come in!" he shouted.

"You're still here," she said, stepping into the kitchen.

"What do you mean, I'm still here? Where else would I be?"

"I mean, you haven't flown the coop yet."

"I see. You expected me to run out on the carnival?"

"Yep."

He turned, displaying a phony surprised expression. "I'm shocked! Me? Run out on an obligation? Even though you *roped* me into it?"

"Yep. Whatcha makin'?"

"Caviar omelet, and don't think a traitor like you has a snowball's chance in Hell of getting any."

"But I'm hungry."

"Why didn't you offer up Drew for the kissing booth?"

"He's a married man. Married men don't kiss women they're not married to."

"A likely story."

"He doesn't have your charisma."

"Flattery will get you nowhere, and stop drooling over my breakfast."

He cracked another egg and scrambled it in the pan. While she watched, he added the sour cream and caviar concoction."

"You making that for me?"

"I hate to eat alone."

She grinned and took out another plate.

After masterly serving the omelet, adding a little parsley as garnish, and pouring two mimosas, Rick sat down.

"Drinking so early?" she asked.

"I'll need it."

"You're not on until eleven."

Rick shuddered. "I can't believe I let you talk me into this."

"I can't either." She chuckled.

"What if some really ugly woman buys twenty-five tickets?"

Mindy shrugged. "Improvise."

"Improvise? That's your answer?" His eyebrows shot up.

She shrugged.

"I'll improvise. I'll drop into a dead faint and have to be carted away. And she'll probably ask for a refund."

Mindy laughed, spraying a touch of her drink on her plate.

"Nice. Now you're spitting on my food."

"Were you always this funny?"

"Of course." A smug smile graced his lips.

"This is delicious," she said, scooping another forkful of food into her mouth.

"You expected anything less?"

"Geez, Rick. You're as arrogant as ever."

"Not really. Just with you. I love how it gets to you."

She gave him a playful slug in the shoulder.

When they finished, she manned the sponge. "I'll clean up. You go change."

"I thought I didn't have to be there until eleven."

"That's when your booth opens. Don't you want to check out the carnival?"

"Seen one carnival, seen them all."

"Right, like you've ever been to one."

"Every year, until I was ten."

"And?" She raised her eyebrows.

"It was magical."

"Get dressed!" She shooed him from the kitchen and went back to her task.

Oliver followed Rick to the second floor. He opened his closet door and rubbed his chin as he contemplated his wardrobe. Breaker Winslow, the king of sexy, knew how to dress to entice the ladies. This was for charity, so he had to pull out all the stops.

He selected a black wife-beater T-shirt and tight black jeans. After a quick shower, he shaved, splashed on *La Nuit*, dressed, and took his time combing his hair. He had to dazzle the ladies, draw them to his booth. He brushed his teeth again and slipped a roll of breath mints into his pocket. Flashing a gleaming smile at himself, he sighed.

"Not like it used to be, Ollie," he said to the pug.

The dog sniffed Rick's foot and sneezed.

"Thanks. I needed that. Your sneezes always bring me good luck. You'll be guarding the house today, boy. Sorry, but I can't bring you with me."

He picked up the pooch and headed for the front door.

A gasp caused him to turn.

"Wow! You look amazing."

"Why, Cousin Mindy. False compliments?"

"No, no, really. I mean it. Damn, Cuz. You're hot."

He chuckled. "That's the idea, isn't it?"

"You'll break all previous records for the carnival."

"As long as I don't get any diseases..."

"Keep your mouth closed and pucker up," she said, heading for her car.

He made a fist. "You'll pay, for this, Ms. Winslow. You'll pay."

THE CARNIVAL WAS BEING held in a large field the town leased every year. It was nine, and set-up crews for the rides were already in motion. Rick stopped to watch as burly men moved machinery and middle-aged couples put together booths to sell their wares.

Some backed their trucks up to their locations and unloaded grills and cooler-after-cooler of meat. Funnels for funnel cakes were placed by make-shift stoves. Slick talkers set up game booths designed to have no winners. Rick narrowed his eyes as he watched men position giant, colorful stuffed animals up front, where small children could drool and pine for prizes never to be won.

He hated the idea that rarely would anyone actually win one of those pink giraffes or blue elephants. Older gents put out the air rifles for the shooting gallery and tennis balls for the knock-down-the bottles game. He remembered how much he'd loved the carnival when he was a kid. His father had taken him every year. They had played all the games, never winning, until once, when his father threw a scowl at the man running the scam and threatened to report him to the sheriff. Little Rick had been amazed at how his father's luck had changed. He'd kept the little blue bear his dad had won until the fire claimed it.

His dad, a tall, sinewy man made his money from sheep, goats, and cows. Honest labor, he'd told his son. They didn't have much, but they ate well, and Rick always had books and a few new clothes for school. When he was young, he didn't know that his father put away a few bucks every week. He kept it in a coffee can in the barn, a place Rick's mother rarely went. By carnival time, his dad had a fair bit of money to burn, and they ate, played games, went on rides, and even had enough left over to buy a souvenir for his mom.

The magic of the carnival had ended for Rick when he turned ten. By then he had modeling dates all summer long because school was out. His mother had told him that they needed to get him out there, to be seen while school was on summer break. His parents had argued incessantly over Rick's career.

Tears stung at the back of his eyes as he remembered those days with Lincoln Winslow, "Linc" to his friends. His father had had a massive heart attack when Rick was in Europe on a photo shoot. He couldn't get back in time for a final goodbye.

At least he had had the satisfaction of making his father's last days easier by funding repairs to the old farmhouse and buying him a new car. Rick's mother sold the place right after his father died. The profit from the sale and Linc's life insurance were enough to buy her a small apartment on the Upper East Side of Manhattan and a new life.

He spied Drew, Mindy's husband, struggling with a wooden structure. One glance at the front, which sported a pair of bright red painted lips with many hearts on a white background, and Rick knew what it was for. He ground his teeth. That must be the kissing booth his cousin-in-law was assembling. Rick ambled over.

"Need a hand?" he asked with his hands in his pockets and a smug smile on his face.

"Would you mind?"

"Yes, I would. Go ahead. Sweat yourself into a coma. Your wife got both of us into this. Now you can feel the pain, just as I'm going to," Rick hissed.

"Hey, look! I told her this was a mistake. I told her you'd be pissed as hell."

"And what did she say?" Rick arched an eyebrow.

"She laughed," Drew said, mopping his face with a handkerchief and not meeting Rick's gaze.

"Sounds about right."

Rick patted Drew on the shoulder. "What do you need me to do?"

"How about getting me some water?"

"That's easy. Be right back."

Rick located a vendor with a giant cooler. He bought three bottles and returned to his booth.

"There you go. It's set up. There are a couple of chairs around here somewhere," Drew said, looking around. "There they are." He retrieved them from behind a tree.

Rick straddled a chair backward and opened his water.

"You got one hot chick in here with you. Ohh, man. That Amber Walker. She's like Miss America," Drew said, gesturing to his chest with cupped hands.

"But she's married, right?"

"Yeah. And her husband's a bruiser with no sense of humor."

"I'll keep my distance."

"I'm bettin' you'll have plenty of women keepin' you busy." Drew snickered, before taking a long drag on the water bottle.

Rick didn't know which he dreaded more, having a lot of women wanting to kiss him or having none.

"We'll see," he said, shrugging. His fear of having no one in line shivered through him.

"Your booth will be the busiest."

"Are you going to buy a ticket for Amber?" Rick turned a harsh eye on him.

"Are you kidding? I like living. Mindy'd skin me alive."

Rick laughed. "Pussy-whipped."

"She's the finest babe in three counties. I may be dense sometimes, but I'm not stupid." He shook his head.

Together the men straightened the old-fashioned sign and dusted off the booth. They placed the chairs in position. It was ten thirty.

"I'm gonna take a look around."

"Yeah, I know. Get your courage up." Drew snickered, placing a box for tickets on the booth's counter.

Rick ignored the growing lump in his stomach and wandered through the carnival. Lured by the smell of hot oil and sugar, he bought a funnel cake. The nostalgic sounds of tinny music joined perfectly with the smell of onions sautéing and cotton candy returning him to his youth. He ambled along to the impressive 4H projects, including the biggest rabbits he'd ever seen. He finished his tour with his favorite carnival treat, a caramel apple. He munched as he returned to his booth. Checking his watch, he barely had time for a trip to the men's room.

With breath freshened, hair combed he manned the booth. Amber was already there.

"Hi, I'm Amber. You're Breaker, right?"

"Rick, to my friends."

They shook hands.

"Ever do this before?" he asked.

"Every year. My dumb-ass sister volunteers me then blackmails me into agreeing."

"You, too? I'm here under duress, too."

She shot him a quizzical look.

"Against my will," he explained.

"Oh, yeah." She nodded.

"Any tips, secrets or anything?"

"Yeah, if someone's got bad breath, make it fast. And don't let the old men touch you. Once they get their hands on your arm, they think that gives them free rein, you know?"

"I'm not exactly worried about that."

"Aren't you going to take your shirt off?" she asked.

"That wasn't part of the deal. I thought this would work," he said, referring to his skimpy tank top.

"It's fine. But bare is better."

He eyed her. "You're buttoned all the way up. No cleavage?"

She shook her head. "These dirty old men don't need encouragement. Last year my husband had to flatten one guy who kept getting 'handy.'"

"Where is he?" Rick glanced around.

"By the men's room. He stands nearby and any guy who gets touchy-feely, he takes care of him."

"What about women?"

"I don't think he'd hit a woman." She chuckled. "You're on your own."

He smiled, but the dread of having no takers grew in his belly.

"Here's a box for the tickets. Don't forget to take 'em. Otherwise, the ladies will just get back in line."

"Are you numb afterward?"

"Yeah. My mouth, my lips. I don't want to kiss my honey for at least half an hour afterward."

"He's a patient man," Rick replied.

"Are you kidding? He's a saint!"

At the sound of a throat clearing, Rick turned away from Amber and almost lost his footing. He again checked his watch. Eleven ten and there must have been a line of ten women in front of his booth.

"Pucker up, Mr. Winslow," said the roly-poly woman with a baby in her arms.

His heart swelled.

"Sweetheart, call me Breaker."

She plunked down five tickets. He put them in the box and closed his hands over her shoulders. "Come here, you luscious thing," he said, bending down to kiss her. After one kiss, she giggled so hard he had to wait to plant the second one. Then he did the other three in quick succession, leaving her breathless.

"There you go, the Fire Department thanks you."

The next woman stepped up. A blonde in her early twenties, he guessed. Nice rack, too. She put two tickets on the counter, her hand trembling. He slid the tickets away, then took her hand in both of his.

"Don't worry, sweetheart. This won't hurt a bit."

She laughed, then leaned in as he bent down.

He couldn't believe how many women clamored to touch his lips. Tall, short, thin, chubby, and downright obese—they all waited patiently for their turn. Most had anywhere from one to five tickets.

The first hour passed in a flash. The shyness and giggles of the women charmed him. He'd never believed how many knew who he was and wanted to kiss him. They simply kept coming, minute after minute, hour after hour, until four o'clock. The business of kissing was thriving.

He stole a glance at Amber's side and the line was just as long. She looked frazzled. Her husband had had to escort two men away from his wife. Her hair was a mess, having been manhandled by dozens of men. She looked ready to quit.

"I'm gonna to close up," she whispered to Rick.

"Only one more hour."

She groaned. He patted her on the back, then stepped back, glancing at her mate, who stared at them. He waved quickly, then resumed his duties.

By now, he'd downed five bottles of water and his lips had begun to tingle a bit. Bracing himself on the counter and shifting his weight to his hands, he gazed down at his feet. Emotion surrounded his heart. He still had fans, dozens of fans. Who would have thunk it?

"Say, buddy. You still in business?" It was a gruff, female voice, but it couldn't fool him. His head snapped up and a smile spread across his face.

There was Dani.

"It's about time. Where the hell have you been?" He pulled the corners of his mouth down in an exaggerated frown.

"Pucker up, Buster." She flashed twenty-five tickets in front of him, waving them back and forth. "Still got a little energy left?" She shot him a flirty look.

"You, my dear, are the fuel that makes the engine run. Come here," he said, grabbing her shoulders. He jerked her toward him and locked lips with her, while his arms held her close. Heat flowed through his veins. The longer he kissed her, the more blood pumped to his dick. Fortunately, the counter was waist high and no one could tell. He didn't give a damn. He was going to kiss Dr. Dani until she knew she'd been kissed.

"Hey, lady. Save some for us!" Came the cry from the crowd lined up behind her. Rick didn't hear anything but the pounding of his heart. Her fingers closed around his biceps, creating pressure and warmth. He swiped his tongue over her lips and she opened for him. He deepened the kiss, his fingers twining in her long hair.

"That's more than twenty-five tickets worth," some woman piped up.

Rick released her. "I agree." She fell back a step, grasping his hand to steady herself.

He gently swept her hair off her face. She trained her beautiful, wide blues on him, her mouth slightly puffy, her lips still open a bit. He cupped her cheek, then placed one final, tender kiss on her lips.

"My turn, my turn. Come on, lady." A large, pushy woman in a plaid dress nudged Dani's arm.

"Of course. Sorry," she mumbled stumbling to the side. Rick stared at her and smiled.

"Who's next?"

"Me!" The round, florid face of the woman in plaid grinned at him.

"What's your name, sweetheart?"

"Blanche."

"Ah, Blanche. A name from the theater."

"I got four tickets."

Rick scooped her tickets off the table and shoved them into the overstuffed box.

"Then you shall have four kisses." He bent down and delivered on his promise.

Blanche blushed to the roots of her hair, chuckled, and turned away to let the next woman have her turn. She stopped, glanced up at Rick and spoke.

"You sure do know how to kiss, Mr. Winslow."

He smiled. Dani stood to the side. After Rick kissed five more women, he turned to her.

"Homer's at six?"

She nodded. He checked his watch.

"Last call! I can take five more, then this booth is closed."

At five to five, Jory Stevens swung around. She announced the kissing booth over. Amber dumped a bottle of water on her head, then pulled out a small towel she'd brought.

"All those hands on me. I need a shower."

"Thank you so much, Amber." Jory hugged her sister.

"Last time I let you talk me into this," Amber said, shooting Jory a dark look.

She took the two boxes, both overflowing with tickets and grinned.

"You two broke the bank. Your booth was the most successful in the entire carnival. We've raised at least five hundred bucks on you two alone. I can't thank you enough."

"You can say that again," Amber moaned, letting her husband rub her hair dry.

"It was more fun than I expected," Rick said.

"Great! Then I'll sign you up for next year."

He raised his palm. "Wait a minute. I don't even know where I'll be next year."

"No problem. I'll be in touch. Thanks again, Breaker. Or do you prefer Rick?"

"Rick."

"You were a good sport to do this."

He smiled and downed one more bottle of water before taking one last stroll through the carnival grounds reviving his memories. The smells of popcorn and cotton candy mixed with meat on the grill, hot oil, and funnel cakes. Canned music, dribbling from loudspeakers, fought for attention with screams from the rides punctuating the air, barkers hooking in suckers, and the din of the crowd.

He reached the parking lot, surprised to be sad to leave. Fighting the lure of the tasty, greasy carnival fare, he hung back. Rick had kept up Breaker's healthy eating habits, except for that one weakness, funnel cake. Now all he wanted was a stiff vodka and tonic or two and a salad.

Rick returned home to walk and feed Oliver before heading to Homer's restaurant on Cedar Lake. The pug circled a dozen times in joy to see his master, his short, curly tail beating the air like a metronome on steroids as Rick put down the food dish. Sweaty and dirty from the heat of the day, Rick rubbed his neck. He needed a shower and fresh clothes, but a lady was waiting—his lady. Who knew what delights might await him after dinner?

Refusing to show up grubby, he made a beeline for the bathroom. Grabbing a washcloth, he scrubbed his face, neck, and head, then took a shot at his underarms. He combed his hair, slapped on a little aftershave and loped to the car. Pressing the pedal closer to the floor, he arrived for his date in no time.

He pulled into the parking lot at Homer's. He exited the car quickly and stopped at the front of the restaurant. The hostess directed him to a table on the deck. After handing him a menu, she stammered and blushed.

"Mr. Winslow, you're a, you're a, a great, you-know."

"Huh?" He raised his brows.

"Great kisser," she blurted out before scurrying away.

"I guess today was a success," Dani said.

"If numb lips are an indication of success, I'm there." He sat across from her.

"Too bad. I had a little project for them after we ate."

He cocked an eyebrow. "Not *that* numb. I'm sure they'll be normal by then."

"Good." She shot him a flirtatious glance.

He checked out the food selection, ordered his drink and a chicken Caesar salad, and sat back staring at Dani. She'd ordered a burger and a beer.

"You look great," he said, his gaze roaming over her.

"You look tired."

"I never knew kissing women would wear me out."

"How many did you kiss?"

He shrugged. "I lost count after twenty."

"Jory Stevens said you broke the bank. Better than even Amber's record."

"Really? She had quite a crowd there."

"Some of the men sneak away to her booth when their wives are occupied."

He laughed. "I can see why."

"Did you sample her?" Dani's brow furrowed.

"Don't be ridiculous. I don't mess with married women. Besides, I was saving up for you."

She chuckled. "That was quite a kiss."

"Twenty-five tickets worth."

The waitress brought their drinks.

"Are you busy after dinner?"

She shook her head.

"I need to shower. I'm a mess," he said after taking a long drink.

"Why don't you shower at my place?"

His eyebrows shot up. "Really?"

"My shower is special. It has something no other shower has," she said, lowering her lashes.

"Oh? Tell me. What could possibly be unique in your shower?"

"Me," she said, raising her gaze to his.

He burst out laughing and took her hand. "Do I need a ticket?"

"Nope."

He leaned over to kiss her. The waitress brought their food, looking first at Rick, then Dani, then back at Rick, and giggling.

"No more tickets. This one is on the house," he said.

The pair couldn't take their eyes off each other while they ate. The more food he consumed, the hungrier he got—for Dani. She matched his stare and ate fast.

Chapter Eight

After dinner, Rick stopped home to pick up his pug. Excited, Dani went straight home. Her nerves were on edge as she tidied up, racing through the house gathering newspapers, dirty laundry, and stopping to wash dishes. Her house would never measure up to the places Rick had been. She chewed her lip while examining her digs.

The two-bedroom cottage attached to the surgery was modest. The small kitchen opened onto a living/dining area. It wasn't meant for a family, but for a single vet, like her. The furniture was clean but well-worn. She'd only been there a short while and had had no time to re-furnish. Besides, she was on probation—sort of. If the old vet recovered and decided to return to his practice, she'd be looking for another job.

Nothing about this job had said *permanent*. She'd taken it after Dean had broken up with her. Figuring the quiet location would give her a chance to sort out her life, she settled in Pine Grove and became a country vet. That was two years ago. Dani had made the transition with no problem. The warm welcome from the community helped heal her heart.

Pine Grove folks had worried about the care of their animals when old Doc Blaine's health failed. The town council debated the question of where they'd find a qualified vet who would accept living behind the clinic and take a whole lot less pay than the big city clinics offered.

Dropped into a place where everyone wanted help with their pet and livestock, but no one wanted to pay, she'd hired Nancy as an ally. The two women calmly, but firmly, insisted on being paid and created a pay scale that worked with the community. Since the lodging was free, Dani could accept lower pay to start.

As she looked around the place, her heart sank. What had appeared comfy now looked shabby. How could she bring a dashing, rich model to this dump? Panic made her sweat, which didn't help her nerves.

Before she could kick herself again for inviting him, the doorbell rang. Too late for second-guessing. She swallowed and gripped the knob. Oliver pushed past Rick, almost knocking him down. The little pug raced into the house, barking. He stopped, lowering his head to sniff every inch of the living room. Dani's cats scooted under the bed.

"Sorry about that. Oliver has no problem making himself at home," Rick said and stepped inside.

"No problem. He's a dog. That's what they do."

The model took her in his arms for a long kiss, melting her fears with his heat. He stood back, his eyes bright with lust.

He ripped his T-shirt over his head. "Now where's that magic shower with the beautiful, naked woman?"

Dani gulped as she stared at his perfect chest. Giving her head a shake, she silently admonished herself to grow up. It's not like she hadn't already slept with the man. But that had been in the dark. And now, well, damn, now she could see the amazing specimen of a man standing before her, taking off his pants. She fanned herself with her hand for a moment, then stopped, embarrassed.

Rick laughed. "Getting hot in here? Damn right. Let's go cool off." He tugged at her shirt. "You're overdressed."

Shyness gripped her. She did not possess a model's body by any means. A little broad in the hips, perhaps, breasts a normal size.

"Oh, no. Don't tell me. You're getting all schoolgirl with me? We've done the deed."

"In the dark," she added.

He chuckled. "You're right. Let's get reacquainted in the light." Wearing only his boxers, he took her hand and led her to the bathroom.

After turning on the water, he removed his underwear and stepped in, holding out a hand to her.

"Come, beautiful lady. Join me."

Her mouth hung open for a second before she recovered. The man was an Adonis. His body was perfection, and she couldn't stop staring. Preoccupied with the man in front of her, she peeled off her clothes. Once completely naked, she took his hand.

"You are incredibly beautiful, Dani," he whispered, brushing his lips against the tender skin beneath her ear.

She wrapped her arms around his waist and lifted her chin. His mouth joined hers as the warm water sprinkled down on them. He had jumpstarted her desire. Fire grew in her veins as he tightened his embrace. She stepped back.

"Clean first," she said, harnessing the wildness in her belly. She picked up the shampoo and motioned for him to bend down. They lathered each other's hair at the same time, laughing and spitting out bubbles.

As she rinsed, Rick rubbed soap on her body. He took care to get every inch of her clean and stoked the flames in her core. When he reached that spot, she spread her legs, giving him better access.

Taking a quick swipe of the soap with her palm, she flattened it against his chest and lathered him up. Pressing her fingers into the hard muscles of his pecs spiked her heartbeat. Touching him was almost as much of a turn on as his caressing her.

As she cleaned him, the fresh scent of her pear soap mixed with his masculine one. It intoxicated her as she breathed in. Gliding her hands down, she cupped him and washed his shaft, which was rock hard.

"Bend over, brace your hands against the wall," he said, his voice ragged.

Glad she'd inserted her diaphragm before he'd arrived, she did as he instructed. He leaned over her back and closed his fingers around her breasts, tweaking the nipples. His tongue swept over her neck. She shivered.

As he stepped closer, she felt his hardness. He dropped one hand off her chest and guided himself to her opening.

"A little wider, baby."

She braced her palms on the wall and moved her feet.

"Now the hips. Stick your butt out."

She did. With one thrust, he entered her.

"Oh, damn!" She shut her eyes as he filled her. He moved his hand to her belly, splaying his fingers out, then ran his hand down, searching. While warm water rained down on her, he touched her gently.

"Oh, Dani, baby, sweetheart," he moaned while his stubble scratched her back. He pumped into her hard and fast. The orgasm rose quickly, coiling inside tighter and tighter. He pinched her nipple one more time and that set off her release, which exploded in her as if he'd lit fireworks inside her body. She groaned loudly, her eyes shut. Needing to touch him, she gripped his hand, holding it in place. She took in a deep breath and let it out slowly.

"Oh, God," he moaned. He snaked his other arm around her middle and clung to her. He gave two more sharp thrusts then stopped.

They held their poses for a moment longer. He kissed the back of her neck.

"Good?" he asked.

Was he insecure? Breaker Winslow could never be insecure about lovemaking. He was almost a pro.

"Amazing," she said.

"Me, too."

They separated, rinsed off, and shut off the water. She reached out for the towels on the rack and offered him a blue one. He wiped his face, swiped it across his hair, then his chest, and fastened it around his waist.

Taking hers, he toweled her hair, then dried her breasts.

"They don't need special attention," she said, reaching for the towel.

"Yes, they do. They told me." He held the fluffy terrycloth away from her.

She laughed. "Whatever. I'm not going to argue."

"Good. Because you wouldn't win."

When he finished drying her, he bent down and kissed each breast. She rested her hands on either side of his head and kissed his hair, then combed it with her fingers.

Once they were dry, he threw on his pants and harnessed Oliver.

"I'll come with you," Dani said, slipping a shift over her head.

He raised his eyebrows. "Nothing underneath?"

She shook her head. "It's dark out."

"But the moon is bright."

"I don't care. Let's go." She took his hand.

Rick led them out into the fresh night air. Dani took a deep breath. Her heart anticipated a long snuggle through the night with the man of her dreams. Ollie trotted along with his nose to the ground. It seemed to take the pooch forever to find a spot to relieve himself.

As they headed back, Rick broke the silence.

"About tonight—" he began.

"You're staying, right?" She cut him off.

In the moonlight, she couldn't see his full face, but a smile crossed his lips.

"Do you want me to?"

"Of course."

"Then I will."

"Did you think I wanted you to go home?"

"Just thought I'd ask."

She snaked her arm around his waist. She couldn't imagine him ever getting tossed out after making love. Disappointment for him, from a woman? She gave her head a slight shake—never. She'd never seen him be insecure.

Inside, they shed their clothes and slipped into bed. He rolled onto his back and stretched out his arm. Within a heartbeat she snuggled into his embrace, resting her head on his shoulder. He tucked her closer.

"I want to spend all night touching you," he whispered, brushing some damp hair from her face.

"Suits me just fine." She sighed.

"Something wrong?"

"Nope. Everything's great."

"You sure?"

"Couldn't be happier." She swallowed the three little words on the tip of her tongue. Damn, there was no way she'd ruin this beautiful night by getting too mushy. Breaker Winslow must have heard hundreds, no, thousands of declarations of love from women—some sincere and some not. She'd be damned if she'd be just one more lovesick lady. She'd already declared her feelings. No reason to beat a dead horse.

Besides, the fastest way to lose a man is to tell him you love him all the time. At least that's what all the magazines said. Nope. She wasn't going there.

"Dani, you've changed my life. Thank you." His declaration was so soft, she wasn't sure she'd heard right.

"You've changed mine, too."

"I have?"

"Confession time."

"Oh, good. And make it juicy," he replied.

"I've had a crush on you for ages."

"Me? You haven't even known me for ages."

"I mean from your pictures. Your book covers. Favorite pastime in airports while waiting for a plane was drooling over your picture. Dean even got a bit jealous."

"Did he say anything when you asked him about the surgery for me?"

She giggled. "Actually, yes."

"What?"

"He said that I'd finally gotten my wish."

Rick laughed. "Did he, really? And what was that wish? To sleep with me?"

"Nothing that bold. Just to kiss you."

He took her chin in his hand and directed her mouth to his.

"There. Just to make sure all dreams are fulfilled."

"You're hilarious." She chuckled.

He pulled the covers up to their shoulders. Oliver jumped up on the bed, circled, and promptly fell asleep. His soft snore cut through the quiet of the night.

"I hope you don't mind," Rick said.

"Not at all. He's welcome on my bed, anytime."

"And me?"

"And you, too."

"Goodnight, darling Dani."

"'Night, Rick."

She let happiness wash through her. Refusing to think about the future, Dani kissed his chest, then closed her eyes, drifting off into a peaceful rest.

RICK OPENED HIS EYES and glanced at the bedside clock. Three o'clock. When he rolled onto his back, his hand came into contact with Dani. Her skin was warm and smooth. His body stirred and so did his heart. He'd never been a spend-the-night kind of guy. Always a love-'em-and-leave-'em type. Models didn't mind. They wanted to get their ten hours of sleep, so they looked good the next day.

A spike of fear shot through him. He didn't want to leave Dani. *I'm not a cuddler.* The rueful smile spreading his lips always appeared when he lied to himself. Though he'd never been much for afterplay, he was now. Turning on his side, he watched her sleep. Her sweet expression touched his heart. He gently brushed at a lock of her hair, easing it away from her face. Then he rubbed it between his fingers. The strands were soft.

She moved closer to him, reaching out. He slid under her arm and scooted up against her. She sighed in her sleep, her palm pressed against his back. How could any man leave this woman, break her heart, and walk away? Anger at Dean welled up inside him, but he tamped it down. He couldn't afford to be hostile toward the man who would try to recreate his looks. Still, he wished he could bash him in the face.

Was her declaration of love sincere? He'd heard it so many times from so many women. Was she simply saying what she thought he wanted to hear? Did Dani have room in her heart for one more? Hope grew inside him. After all, she'd invited him to stay over. And he'd broken every one of his rules to do it, too. He prayed Dr. Welling could heal his outside, and that Dr. Dani could take care of the inside. So far, she had done a fantastic job. Happiness and peace rolled through him like ripples at low tide. She turned over, and he spooned her. Sleep returned before his dick could protest.

The feel of warm flesh and a hard nipple pressing into his back woke Rick. This time the clock showed eight and sun streamed in the windows. A feminine arm wrapped around his waist. He closed his fingers over it to keep her against him.

"Better than an alarm clock," he muttered.

A sleepy sound came from the woman he couldn't see. He lifted her fingers to his lips and heard a moan.

"Hmm. Could you wake me up like this every day?" Her sleepy voice broke the quiet.

He froze. Did she mean she wanted him there every day? Was that love? Had he ever experienced real love? He doubted it. Would he know it if he did? He wasn't sure.

"That could be arranged," he responded, then held his breath for a second.

Warm lips tickling the back of his neck gave him the answer. He shivered and laughed. She hitched her leg over his hip and growled in his ear.

"You treat wolves, too?" he asked.

"You're the only one."

"Very funny," he said, attempting to sound serious. The giggling behind him put a smile on his face.

"I thought it was."

He rolled over and ran his fingers through her hair. "God, you look great," he said.

"Oh my God. No, I don't." She covered her face with her hands.

He pulled them away and kissed her nose, then brushed her lips with his. He scooped her into his arms and lay back on the bed. Dani rested her cheek on his chest. Rick felt something move.

"Uh oh."

"What?" she asked.

"You asked for it. And here it comes."

As the snorting got closer, Dani's eyes widened. Within a few seconds, a hot, wet pug tongue was cleaning her face. Laughter amid the shrieks had Rick doubled over.

"You said he could sleep here."

"Sleep here, not give me a bath," she said, hiding under the covers.

"It's time to take him out. Let's go." He tugged the blankets down. A grinning Oliver stared at her.

Dani threw back the covers and raced to the bathroom, with a barking dog at her heels. Laughter seeped through the closed door. Oliver stood sentinel, waiting for her to emerge.

Rick vaulted out of bed and threw on his boxers and pants. When the door opened, he pulled his shirt over his head.

"Damn. You're spoiling the view," she said, tying her robe.

"Throw something on. Let's take him out."

She eased a shift over her naked body and slipped her feet into flip-flops. Rick harnessed the pooch.

"Let me put the coffee on and I'll join you."

He nodded as he opened the door. The clinic was backed by about a quarter of an acre of lawn that met dense woods. Rick turned a sharp eye to the trees, looking for bears and coyotes. Finding none, he let out the retractable leash a little farther, giving Oliver more freedom.

Someone came up behind him, threading their arms through his, hugging his middle.

"Dani?"

"You expected the Queen of England?"

He turned, slinging an arm around her shoulders.

"Doing anything today?" she asked.

"Nope. No plans. Just recovering from the kissing booth."

"Stay. I'll make breakfast, then take you to meet the horses."

"Oliver invited, too?"

"Of course."

"An offer I can't refuse."

The pug spied Dani and ran up to her, jumping up on her leg. Rick admonished the dog and eased him down.

"Guess he likes you as much as I do."

"Do you like me as much as he does?"

"More. And I saw you first, but don't tell Ollie."

"Let's go eat."

"What's for breakfast?"

"I make a mean bacon and eggs."

Rick whistled for the dog and the three of them returned to the house.

AFTER BREAKFAST, RICK did the dishes. Dani came up behind him at the sink and hugged him.

"I have to change before we go see the horses."

Rick slid his hand up and down her arm. "Why don't I come with you?"

"Why?"

"Why not?" His lifted her hand to his mouth.

"Oh. I see," she replied.

"Interested?"

"Very."

As soon as he dried his hands, she led him to the bedroom where they made love. A quick group shower before getting dressed gave him the opportunity to take her again, which he did.

"Let's take my car," she said, offering him her hand as they headed for the door.

He fastened Oliver in the backseat and climbed in next to the vet. They rode out to the farm where the two horses lived. Dani introduced Rick, who hung back. Oliver was downright hostile. He barked and barked at the horses. They ignored him, eying Rick with curiosity. Rick calmed the dog. He lifted the pug and brought him over to touch and sniff the big beasts.

"You've dealt with the toughest agents, publishers, and ad people in New York City, but you're afraid of a horse?"

"New Yorkers don't have such big teeth and hooves," he said.

Rick passed on the offer to ride but did offer a few apples to the pair. They vied for his attention, flattering him. As the visit drew to a close, Rick insisted on taking Dani to dinner. After dropping Oliver at home, they picked up his car and drove to Homer's. As the night rolled in, the air chilled. They selected seats inside.

They ordered burgers. Rick drew the line at fries and ordered a side salad instead. As they ate, a touch of sadness washed through him. He'd be going home alone tonight. Tomorrow, Dani had a full morning at the clinic, then an afternoon of inoculating livestock. He couldn't ask her to spend the night again, yet he didn't want to leave her. Was this love? He guessed it must be.

"How about next weekend?" Rick asked, digging into his salad.

"What about next weekend?"

"Spend it with me. And every weekend for, until, maybe forever?"

She choked on her food. Rick jumped up and was at her side, pounding her back until she waved him off.

"I'm okay." She reached for her water glass.

Rick took his seat, watching her. Dani coughed once more and cleared her throat.

"Did you mean it?"

"What?"

"Every weekend?" she replied.

He nodded. *What the hell am I doing?*

A peachy blush suffused her cheeks. "Sounds good to me."

Rick swallowed. What had he gotten himself into? "Good. Let's start with this weekend."

"Your place or mine?"

He rubbed his chin and thought for a moment. "Alternate. Let's alternate."

She raised her glass. "To weekend lovers," she said.

He clinked his with hers. "Lovers."

Worrisome thoughts went out of his head and his smile wouldn't quit.

"Maybe I'll have fries, too," he said and motioned for the waitress.

When they had finished dinner, he returned home to Oliver. The house was quiet. Next weekend, Dani would be staying there. Panic seized him. Rick had never lived with a woman. Sure, he'd had plenty in his bed, revolving in and out of his social life, but no one ever hung a toothbrush in his bathroom before. He had no idea what to do. He dialed his cousin, Mindy.

"Well, well, if it isn't hot lips Casanova. I heard you were the hit of the carnival."

"Not now, Mindy. I need help."

"What's wrong?"

"Dani's coming here. Next weekend. To stay. For the whole weekend."

"Congratulations, Master Lothario. She's some catch."

"I mean staying here. In my house."

"You've never had a woman sleep over before? Why is that hard to believe?" She snorted.

"Very ladylike, Mindy."

"Really, you haven't?"

"I preferred they not spend the night. A few have slipped through. But I got rid of them in the morning. No one has ever moved in, even for two days—until now."

"Panic-stricken?"

"Terrified. What do I do? I have no clue."

"First, empty out a drawer. Second, start practicing putting down the toilet seat."

"Be serious."

"I am. Dead serious. If she falls into the toilet in the middle of the night, your romance may be over."

"She's not that superficial."

"Try falling in the toilet at three a.m., Rick."

"Okay, okay. I get it. Put the seat down. And clean out a drawer?"

"And have some empty hangers for her, too."

"In my closet?"

"Of course, in *your* closet."

"Okay. Wait. Let me get a piece of paper. I think I need to write this down."

Mindy chuckled.

"Laugh all you want. This is important. I love her and don't want to fuck it up."

"Oh my God. You're serious. Serious about her?"

"I guess you could say that."

"This is a first. Should I alert the media?"

"Stop it," he snapped.

"Okay. All right. Hey, she's a great choice. Someone smart enough not to take crap from you."

"Your flattery overwhelms me."

"Now that I think of it, you two are a good match. I'm happy for you, Rick."

His tone softened. "Thanks."

"Are you happy?"

"First time in a long time. Maybe ever."

"That's wonderful. You deserve it after everything."

"Thanks. Continue with the things I need to do," he said, cradling the phone as he picked up a pen.

"Remember to close the door when you go into the bathroom," she said.

"Don't be ridiculous."

"Just beginning at the beginning."

Chapter Nine

Friday night, after the clinic closed, Dr. Dani Henderson turned into Rick Winslow's driveway. She peeked in the rearview mirror while she refreshed her lipstick. Nerves jangled as she sat in her car. What was she doing here? Spending the weekend with world-famous playboy extraordinaire, Breaker Winslow? She was probably the first veterinarian he'd bedded. Would he be striking *screwing a female vet* off his bucket list?

Shame filled her. Whatever the media had written about him might have been true before the fire, but she knew a different man. When she thought of him, adjectives like brash, outspoken, selfish, but also kind, generous, and funny came to mind. And honest—to a fault.

She'd agreed to do this, although she almost choked to death when he had asked. What would her parents say if they could see her? After her mother got over being jealous, she'd probably tell Dani to follow her heart—and that's what she was doing, wasn't she?

She rested her forehead against the steering wheel. Would Rick turn out to be another Dean? Would he walk away and crush her without so much as a look back? Fear spiked in her chest. Her mind screamed at her to run as fast as she could. But it was too late. She'd given him her heart, even though he didn't know it yet, and there was no getting it back.

A sudden tap on the window made Dani nearly jump out of her skin.

"Are you all right?" It was Rick, his brows drawn together.

She took a breath and managed to smile. "I'm fine."

"Are you going to come in? Or sit out here all night. I don't bite. I promise."

She opened the door, swung her legs around, and pushed to her feet. A click of her keys opened the trunk.

"This it?" he asked, picking up a small overnight bag.

She nodded. He slung an arm around her shoulders and steered her toward the front door.

"You're not afraid of me, are you?"

"Of course not. I don't usually sleep with men who scare me." *I'm terrified, but not the way you think.*

"Good. I've made some changes," he said, opening the door.

Dani was greeted with several barks from Oliver as he jumped up against her leg, trying to lick her face. She laughed and knelt down to give the pug his chance.

"God, he's just the cutest thing, Rick."

"I thought I was." He made a pouty face.

She swiped playfully at his shoulder.

"This way," he said.

She followed him into the bedroom. Her mouth hung open. Not the big empty room she'd seen before. The room was fully decorated, and airy, with windows on two walls. The bed was a king with a hand-made patchwork quilt in blues, greens, and white. The walls were a minty green with white trim on the windows. There were two oak dressers. Country scenes in oils hung on the walls and a rag rug covered much of the newly-refinished oak floor. There were two nightstands with white milk-glass lamps and white shades.

"This is for you," he said, opening an empty drawer. "And I have a dozen hangers waiting for you in the closet." He opened the door to show her.

"I'm impressed."

He gave a short bow. "Anything for my lady."

"Am I your lady?"

"Every weekend."

She sighed, wishing he'd said more.

"Why don't you unpack? I'll make drinks. Dinner is simmering."

"Dinner?"

"Okay, I didn't make it. Jess Lennox did. It's stew. She's a pretty good cook. Whole lot better than me."

"I didn't expect you to cook dinner. Guess I thought we'd throw together sandwiches or I'd make eggs."

"Tomorrow morning, I'm making my famous pancakes."

She raised her eyebrows. "Really?"

"You'll love 'em. Now finish up here. I'm hungry." With that, he left the room.

Dani put her clothes away, pushing aside a feeling of weirdness to have her things in the drawer next to his. After everything was put away, she descended the stairs slowly. She loved this old farmhouse. Rick had hired Will Lennox to renovate it. He hadn't finished, but the first floor and Rick's bedroom were done. The house was gorgeous. She'd describe it as country chic. She'd never dated a man with such elegant taste, he almost made her feel dowdy.

"I mixed this Cosmo just the way you like it, on the sweet side," he said, handing her a glass.

She took a sip and eased down the on the milk chocolate brown sofa next to him.

"It's perfect," she said, taking another taste.

"Like you," he said and raised his glass. "Here's to the first of many great weekends."

She clinked with him and smiled. He'd made her feel welcome, which was more than she had expected. Perhaps she'd finally find her happy ending with this sexy man?

Later that night, after they made love, she lay, naked, next to him in the big bed. It was late, and she'd dozed but the hoot of an owl woke her up. Rick, also bare, slept quietly next to her. She rolled over to gaze at him. His hair hung over his forehead. She touched his shoulder, and he rolled onto his back.

Dani seized the chance to cuddle up to him. In his sleep, he muttered something and pulled her closer. She drank in his masculine scent combined with the warmth of the bedclothes. The heat from his body shielded her from the cool night air. She pulled the lightweight blanket up to her shoulder and rested her palm on his chest.

His hard body and soft skin inspired passion. An excellent lover, so far beyond her expectations, she had achieved new plateaus of sexual pleasure with him. Touching him, snuggling into his embrace, gave her the sense of safety she needed to drift off to sleep again.

THE REST OF THE WEEKEND flew by. Rick and Dani spent time preparing the barn for the horses. He pulled out a cookbook and, together, they tried a new recipe for a squash casserole with meat. With the new recipe, there were several missteps that led to raucous laughter and do-overs.

Rick had had a compartmentalized life. Women as friends were never lovers, and women who were lovers were never friends. He'd been confused, amazed, and pleased that he'd found both in one woman. The sheer economy of an all-around woman appealed to his practical side.

Fear gripped him. If she had everything, maybe he'd have to marry her. The thought scared him so badly he was almost physically ill. Marriage was for other people. People who wanted kids, families, houses, mortgages—those people got married. Not superstars like Breaker Winslow. He'd never marry. He'd vowed to go on modeling forever, morphing into the senior market when he got older. He'd never stop working, never stop living the good life and never marry. Until the fire sent his dreams up in smoke.

On Tuesdays, he found himself wishing it was Friday. He'd talked to Oliver about Dani. The pug was her biggest fan. On Sunday mornings, the animal licked her face first. They'd rise and walk him together. Rick awoke smiling on those days because she was there. Who was this person, this mellow man? It couldn't be the famous Breaker Winslow, stone-cold heart-breaker?

On Friday, he got a phone call. When he hung up, his hand shook, and a lump formed in his stomach. He'd save it to tell Dani that night. They would be at his house again. He'd made lasagna for dinner. Mixing up a batch of Cosmos, he thought about the news he had to deliver. Excitement tingled through him. Before he could get further lost in thought, the doorbell rang. It was her.

After it banged open, he blurted out, "I've got news."

"Good news?"

He nodded. "Come in, come in."

She sat on the sofa, staring at him.

"Cosmo?"

She nodded.

He poured two drinks and carried them to the couch.

"Well? Aren't you going to tell me?"

"Okay," he said, taking a breath. "I got a call from Dr. Welling's office. They've had a cancellation. They can take me in two weeks."

Her eyes widened.

"Don't you see how great that is? I might look like a normal man in two weeks."

"You look like a normal man now."

"You know what I mean." He jumped and paced.

She simply stared.

"Aren't you going to congratulate me? Don't you want me to have the procedure? That's what she called it. Not surgery. A procedure. Sounds so much easier." He stopped.

"I want whatever makes you happy." Dani shifted in her seat and crossed her legs.

"This is it. This makes me very happy."

"Good. Then let's toast." She raised her glass, but her eyes didn't smile. "To a successful procedure in two weeks."

He clinked his against hers. "You don't seem happy." His eyes narrowed.

"I'm not sure this is going to give you what you want."

"Neither am I. But it's going to get me closer than staring into space."

"True." She nodded, but he wasn't convinced.

"Do you love me, Dani?" His heart had risen to his throat. *Put it all out there, jerk, so she can shoot you down.*

She choked on her beverage for a second. "Leave it to you to get right to the point."

"Well, do you?"

"Yes. You know that."

"I don't. Not if you don't tell me. Then if you do, be happy for me. This won't raise Breaker Winslow from the dead, but it'll do a lot to make looking in the mirror less painful."

She touched his forearm. "I'm being insensitive. Of course, it will. I am happy for you, Rick. I want whatever you want."

He leaned over and kissed her. "Oh, by the way, I love you, too."

"Knew it," she quipped, grinning. "Something smells good. Have you spent the day bending over a hot stove?"

"How did you know? I've been slaving away just to impress you."

"And what did you make?"

"Lasagna. Don't know how good it is. It's my first attempt," he said then finished his drink.

"I'm sure it's great. I'm hungry. Let's go." She rose up and offered her hand.

"We'll see if you still love me after you eat," he said as he joined her.

DANI ROLLED OVER AND woke up at four in the morning. She eased out of bed, trying not to wake Rick. She slipped on his robe because she liked the scent of him and padded to the window. Sliding the curtain to the side, she peered out on the back of his property. Her gaze rested on the barn.

Dani had fantasized about life in Rick's world. What would it be like to live there fulltime? The barn conjured up images of horses, hay, and saddles. There was plenty of room for a riding ring, all it needed was fencing.

The ragtag former chicken coop would be her next project. Would Rick risk going into that moldy, smelly place and cleaning it out? Did he really want chickens or was he simply pulling her leg? Chickens. She'd always wanted chickens. Fresh eggs tasted so much better than store-bought ones.

She turned her thoughts to his news. In two weeks, they'd know if his face could be returned to its former gorgeousness. She doubted he'd get his modeling looks back. Would he be devastated if the procedure didn't give much improvement? She'd be there to help him pick up the pieces and get back to life in sleepy Pine Grove.

A smile played at her lips. She had a chance of having it all with him. He said he loved her and had proved it both in and out of bed. Always glad to see her, he'd open the door and start chattering on about something while he fussed in the kitchen and poured wine like water. There was a warmth about his house, it welcomed her.

Mrs. Rick Winslow. Mrs. Breaker Winslow. She frowned. The first one sent electricity through her, the second one grabbed her heart and squeezed. She didn't want to be Mrs. Breaker Winslow. *Leave Breaker in the grave, where he belongs.* She let out a breath. Chances of that happening were one in a million. She bet he'd get some improvement in his looks, but no way could he go back to what he had been before the fire.

That thought, which would upset him, comforted her. He'd rant and rave, probably threaten to sue Dean, but in the end, she'd be there to help him adjust to reality. His vibrant energy and irreverent attitude stimulated her. He challenged her intellect, her taste, and her judgment. Convinced she was a better version of herself around Rick, she craved his company.

She'd adjusted to weekends with him easily. Being in love suited her—it added a touch of brilliance to the colors and emotions in her life. And the sex was fantastic. She sneaked downstairs, tiptoeing past the snoring pug, who raised his head, then went back to sleep, to curl up on the sofa with pen and paper. They'd have two more weeks together before he went off to the clinic in California. She made a list of things for them to do together before he left. At five, she rested her head on the arm of the couch and fell asleep.

"There you are," Rick said, his hands on his hips.

Dani yawned and opened her eyes.

"I woke up and you were gone. Scared the shit out of me. Don't do that."

"I'm sorry. I couldn't sleep so I came downstairs. I made a list of all the things we should do before you go to California," she said as she handed him the paper.

He eased down on the arm of the sofa. "County Fair. Ice cream at the Creamery. Dinner at Chef's Table in Oak Bluffs. Settle horses in the barn. Clean up chicken coop...what?"

"Yep. Fresh eggs are the best."

"You want me to get chickens? I can barely deal with the idea of a horse or two."

"Chickens are easy."

"Yes, when I'm tending them." He cocked an eyebrow at her.

"I'll help."

"On weekends," he muttered.

Unless we get married. She slapped her hand over her mouth before realizing she hadn't said it out loud.

"What?"

"Nothing."

"Don't play that game with me." He lunged at her, trapping her beneath him and tickled her until she screamed with laughter. Then he kissed her. He raised his head to allow her to catch her breath and then kissed her again. She wound her arms around his neck and pressed up against him.

"Never done it on this sofa. Let's break it in," he said, his voice heavy with desire.

She giggled when he slid his hands under her gown.

TIME PASSED FASTER than Rick expected. They hadn't done everything on Dani's list. Tonight, he was taking her for their last dinner out, and he could cross Chef's Table off the list. Since he had no clue where Oak Bend was, Dani picked him up.

"I've hired Will to do the chicken coop after he's finished with everything else."

"That will be some time next year," she quipped.

"The barn was bad enough. The chicken coop is beyond consideration."

"Will's a good guy. I'm sure he'll get to it."

"Do we have to go shopping for chickens?" he asked.

"You can come. Or I can do it, if you want."

"I've never shopped for chickens. It might be fun."

She reached over and squeezed his hand.

Rick tried to focus on Dani's words, but his mind kept wandering. The limo to drive him to Kennedy Airport would arrive the next morning at ten. By one, he'd be winging his way west, taking the biggest chance of his life. Fear, nerves, and dread gathered in his belly, sending his appetite south.

"You're not eating?" she asked, taking a bite of her chicken parmigiana.

He pushed his plate away. "I'm not hungry."

"We'll take the steak to go, please," Dani said to the waiter. He nodded.

"Let's just leave it."

"You'll probably be starving by midnight."

He shrugged. Nothing mattered. He simply needed to get this procedure over with and get his life back. Everything rode on the success of doctors he'd never met. They told him to be prepared to stay for a month. They had to do tests before the procedure and monitor him afterward. Dani had agreed to keep Oliver while he was away.

"I feel better knowing Ollie will be watching over you while I'm gone. I've trained him to bite the balls off any naked man he sees in your house."

Dani clapped her hand over her mouth to keep from spitting out her food.

"You're welcome to stay at my place, too," he said.

"I might need to. If I get the horses, I'll bunk in at your house while they're in your barn."

"Sounds like a good idea. Ollie will probably be more comfortable there, too. Then he won't think I've given him away."

"Right."

She sighed and returned her gaze to her plate. He'd never seen her so subdued before. He didn't know what to make of it. Was she sad to see him go? A small smile crept across his face as he thought of the final item he'd added to her list—mentally. There was one more thing he needed to do before he left. Perhaps the proposal should wait until he returned. He frowned. What if the doctors fucked up the procedure and he came out worse than when he went in? A scowl washed over him like high tide.

"What's the matter?" she asked.

He shook his head.

"Come on. Fess up," she coaxed.

"Okay." He took a deep breath. "What if they mess it up and I come out looking like Quasimodo?"

"That could never happen. Worst case scenario would be that they can't fix the scars. But they would never make you worse, as you put it."

"I'm glad one of us is confident." He took a swallow of wine.

They finished eating. The waiter packed up the steak, Rick paid the bill, and they headed home. He double-checked his suitcase, then headed for bed. Dani tagged along behind.

He turned, enveloping her in his arms. "Wanna make love? Last call for a month."

"You have to ask?" She wound her arms around his waist and raised her chin for his kiss.

After they finished, and he'd flipped off the light, she cuddled into him. He drew her close, his fingers caressing her bare skin.

"No matter what happens, I love you, Dani."

"I love you, too. I'm sure it'll be fine."

Her vow soothed him.

"Sometimes things happen. Bad things. I mean with anesthetic and, well, you know."

"Nothing like that is going to happen to you." Her tone was crisp.

"Of course not."

He closed his eyes, but sleep wouldn't come. He'd never felt more wide awake in his life. He buried his nose in her hair, relishing the fresh scent of pears. Nerves about the procedure warred with the contentment in his heart. So, this is what love felt like? He tried to push thoughts about the surgery away and focus on the lovely woman in his arms.

Rick's former idea of sharing a bed with a woman didn't go past two in the morning. Certain that waking up alone was the best possible outcome, he'd managed to keep out overnight guests. Dani had changed everything. Waking up to find her there warm, soft, and willing was beyond his wildest dreams. Someone to share a glass of warm milk with when he couldn't sleep. Or something more intimate. Sex was his favorite sleeping pill.

He'd never known a woman like Dani—a woman not obsessed with her looks, or the price and status of things. Finding a woman so unselfish who could tolerate him had been a challenge. And now he'd found her. What if something went wrong? What if he died during the surgery? What would happen to Dani, to the dream of their life together? He shivered at the idea.

She hugged him in her sleep, murmuring something he couldn't understand. Perhaps he should simply consider himself the luckiest man on Earth, stop second-guessing life, and go to sleep. So that's what he did.

DANI SENSED A STRANGE awkwardness at breakfast the next morning. Rick's sarcastic veneer had disappeared. He ate his bacon and eggs quietly, throwing her a soulful look from time to time. Oliver barked a few times and circled Rick. She smiled. Even the dog knew something was up.

"You have Oliver's feeding and walking schedule?" Rick asked.

"I do."

"And his bath schedule."

"I can take care of him, Rick."

"I know, I know. Sorry. Just on edge."

She reached across the table and squeezed his hand. "It's okay. I'm not you, but I'll be the next best thing."

A wan smile curled his lips for a moment. "I'll miss him. And you. Of course, you."

She laughed. "Just don't sleep with anyone else, okay?"

"Who me? I'll look like Frankenstein. Who'd sleep with me?"

She cocked an eyebrow.

"Okay, okay. You don't have to worry," he reassured her.

They finished eating and then she cleaned up while he finished packing. He didn't need much but took a full suitcase anyway.

"Stay here, Dani. Stay in the house. Please."

"I will. It's best to be here to take care of the horses."

A horn honk drew their attention. Her gaze went to the front window. The limo driver was heading up the walk.

"It's time," she said. Tears stung her eyes.

"Yep." He pulled her to him for a quick, hard hug, then kissed her. The doorbell rang.

Rick opened it, greeted the driver, and handed him the bag.

"Good luck," she said, fighting to keep her voice even and losing. Dani stood in the doorway, leaning against the jamb. She prayed nothing went wrong. What if he returned more scarred than when he went? What if he died? If Dean screwed this up, she'd kill him. As the vehicle pulled out of the driveway, she raised her hand, while keeping a firm grip on the pug who tugged to run after his master. Rick looked out the back window and returned her farewell.

A sense of emptiness shot through her as she backed into the house and shut the door. Oliver gave a howl that shook her to her bones.

"Yes, Ollie. I feel the same way," she said, returning to the dishes in the sink.

Once she'd cleaned up, she unpacked the valise she'd brought. Sleeping in Rick's bed would make his absence easier to take. She made the bed, stopping to run her palm over his pillow. She blew out a breath, took a shower, and bundled Oliver into her car. Then she headed for the clinic. Work was the best thing.

"Morning," Dani said, hoping to appear professional as she led Oliver into the waiting room.

"Is it?" Nancy cocked an eyebrow.

Dani stopped dead. "What do you mean?"

"Didn't one male model wing his way west to get his face fixed?"

Dani gasped. "Where did you hear that?"

"Everyone's talking about it."

"Rick would kill if he knew that. He's a very private person."

"Wasn't so private while he was spreading saliva in that kissing booth."

"By the way, I saw you in line. So, don't try to pretend you didn't pucker up, Nancy." Dani grinned as her assistant turned as pink as bubble gum.

"I only got one ticket before the booth closed," she complained.

"I'll have Rick reserve some for you when he gets back," Dani said.

Nancy blushed and waved her hand. "Silly!"

"What's up today?"

Nancy rattled off the schedule. Dani retrieved her white coat and stethoscope and returned to the waiting room. She planted Oliver by Nancy's side. The first patient had arrived. Glad to be busy, she pushed thoughts about Rick Winslow out of her mind and focused on the animals in her care. At lunch, she sat with Nancy and Oliver while she ate her sandwich and compared notes from the morning.

"Are we booked for the next few days?" Dani asked.

"Yep."

"Good. Schedule patients for every available time."

"Don't want any downtime, hmm? Gotcha, Doc. I'll take care of it."

Dani started office hours at eight and stayed on the job until eight at night. Sometimes, she'd treat emergency patients even later. Afterward, she'd walk Oliver. Then the Doc and the pooch would fall into bed, exhausted.

Rick had called after checking into the clinic.

"They're making me wait, like maybe four days, before they do the thing."

"They have to do tests, Rick. Be patient."

"And they're getting ready to take a ton of pictures. Some Dr. Welling said were for the surgery and some for before-and-after."

"That's right."

"Oh, Dr. Welling said to tell you hello."

"Really?"

"Yeah. I wanted to tell him to drop dead, but not until after I'm whole again."

She laughed. "Not necessary."

"Do you still care for him?

"I have you. Why would I need him?"

"I miss you."

"Me, too. But I'm keeping busy."

"I feel like Dracula. There are no mirrors here."

"That's on purpose."

"Okay. Someone's at the door. Gotta go. Love you," he said.

"Love you, too." She hung up and slid into bed, after uttering a few prayers for her lover.

Chapter Ten

Rick woke up groggy and nauseous. A nurse attended him the minute he stirred. She explained that the doctor would be in to see him in an hour and then she brought him some ice chips to quench his thirst. He touched his face, but it was bandaged. Curiosity poked at him the way a boy with a stick jabs at a frog.

"I'm sorry, Mr. Winslow, I can't tell you anything. You'll have to wait for the doctor."

The hour crawled by like a slug in a garden. He had to know, had to see what he looked like. Finally, the doctor arrived.

"How are you feeling, Rick?" Dr. Welling asked.

"Fine. How'd it go? What do I look like?"

Dean chuckled. "I know you're anxious to know the outcome. We thought the procedure went well. But we have yet to see how it will heal. We need to give it time."

"Come on. You've been through this before. Give me some idea."

"This isn't a rote thing. People heal differently. We'll have to wait and see. I know you don't want to hear that, but I can't give you anything definitive now."

"But you're hopeful?"

"Very hopeful. Your skin is good and you're young enough. We're expecting a full recovery and a significant improvement."

Rick smiled. "Good. Thanks." He shook the doctor's hand.

"Now comes the hard part. Waiting for the healing to begin."

"And I have to stay for three weeks?"

"Yes. Maybe longer. Depends on how it goes. Get a good night's sleep. This doesn't happen in the blink of an eye. It's a process."

The doctor left and the nurse arrived. So did Rick's dinner. He cast a jaundiced eye at the plate of mush.

"God, am I going to have to eat this crap for three weeks?"

"Unless you heal faster and get out of here sooner."

"Ugh."

The nurse pushed aside the tray and applied cold packs to Rick's face to reduce the swelling.

"What's the drill?" he asked.

"This will be on for two minutes and off for five for the next four hours."

"Okay. Let's go," he said. *I've come this far, I'm not going to fuck it up now.*

Doctors checked his face every day. Nurses removed the bandages, applied healing medication, including vitamin E, and rebandaged twice a day. Between the ice packs and the treatments, he didn't have much time to rest.

"You're making good progress, Rick. Things are looking good," Dr. Welling said.

"You think it worked?"

The doctor nodded.

"Good. Will I be the way I was?"

"Not completely, but we're guessing you'll be close."

Close? He'd accept close—a whole lot better than Quasimodo. Rick grinned. He couldn't wait to call Dani.

"How are you?" The concern was evident in her tone.

"Great! The doc said I'd be close to my old self."

"How do you feel?"

"Sore, swollen, weird. But it'll be worth it."

"Have you seen your face yet?"

"They don't allow you in a room with a mirror until they think you're ready."

"Oh, okay. Makes sense."

"Dr. Welling is a nice guy."

There was a pause.

"If you're a patient," Dani clarified.

"Right. Right. Not like I'd like you to go out with him again."

"Not like that's going to happen."

"Right," he agreed.

"How much longer do you think you'll be there?"

"They said it depends on the healing. How are things at home?"

"Fine. The horses are loving your barn. Will has started work on the chicken coop."

"How's Ollie?"

"Missing you. He moped around for the first few days. But he's adjusted."

"You mean, now, he's your dog?" His voice rose, and he sat up straight.

"Of course not. He'll go crazy when you get back. I know he misses you."

"Why? Did he say so? You're making that up."

"I'm not. Dogs remember. I know he'll remember your scent."

"Good, because my face will be different."

"Gotta go. Time to feed the mares."

"Don't find anyone else while I'm gone."

"If Prince Charming pops out of the woodwork, you're history."

He laughed. "Okay. I get it. Love you, Dani."

"Love you, too."

He hung up and rubbed the back of his neck. Was he imagining things or did she pull back when he said he'd look different? Would they be over if his looks returned? Nah, no way—not Dani. She's the one who went to bat for him with Dr. Welling. He picked up the television remote and channel surfed, looking for something to hold his attention.

He stopped when he saw Tiffany Cowles, editor-in-chief of *Celebs 'R Us*. She had her own half-hour talk show. Hmm, if he really did regain his looks that might be the perfect place to have an interview and give old Doc Welling some well-deserved publicity. He left the TV there and watched the program.

DANI SIGHED. THOUGH overjoyed to find out that Rick was okay, she worried. If he got his looks back, would he still be interested in her? Women would be falling all over themselves to get his attention. Even with the slight disfigurement he had, the line for the kissing booth at the carnival had been around the block.

She didn't relish the competition. Always ready to face academic and performance-based competition growing up, Dani had been shy about vying with other women for the attention of a man. She'd never entered into a battle for a guy. She'd simply shrugged and walked away, figuring there'd always be another attractive fellow to draw her eye.

This might be different. Already totally in love with Rick Winslow, how would she handle other women trying to break that up? Not well. Of course, it would depend on his reaction. Men who encouraged women to fight for them turned her off, though Rick seemed the opposite. He'd been burned by more than the flames of the blaze. He'd lost his friends and admirers. She had to believe his cynical attitude would prevail. Not a man easily fooled, especially after the fire, he wouldn't be swept off his feet by a burst of female attention, would he?

She breathed out and in. She and Rick were solid, and she had to be happy for his return to his former looks. As she headed for the barn, Dani turned her thoughts to the horses. Without Rick's generosity, these horses might have been destroyed or dumped in a horse rescue.

Instead, they were thriving. Will had made the fence a priority and the spanking new, natural wood rails enclosed a generous paddock.

On her lunch break, Dani saddled up the bay and put a lead on the chestnut. She'd ride the bay about for a while and leave the chestnut in the paddock to graze. The horses were best friends and needed to be together at all times.

The doctor enjoyed riding. When she was eight, Dani had dreamt of having her own horse. One reason she snapped up the vet job in Pine Grove was the opportunity to work with horses. No way would that come her way in the big city.

She gazed at the back of the farmhouse as the horse took a turn, paralleling the fence. Rick's place had grown splendid under the care of Will Lennox. It made her little box behind the clinic seem less than inadequate. The cramped pre-fab, with small windows, was more like a shanty.

She spread out in Rick's large bed every night, missing him, but enjoying the luxury. She hadn't been raised in fancy surroundings, and her parents were smart but ordinary people with zero pretensions. Rick Winslow had introduced her to the good life. Although it seemed like a fairytale at first, she'd grown accustomed to comfort and beauty. When he returned, it would be a huge comedown to return to her former, spare life in the apartment behind her office.

She sighed. Time to enjoy it while she could. After riding, she wiped down the horses and left them outside to enjoy the sun and grass. She filled the trough with water and went inside to shower and return to the clinic.

Leaving the clinic at eight, Dani drove to the house, bedded the horses down for the night and heated up some leftovers for a late dinner. Rick called.

"The fucking food here sucks. I wouldn't feed it to Oliver."

"You only have about two weeks left there."

"I don't care. This stuff is disgusting. Soup from a can. I know when it's soup from a can!"

"Rick! Calm down. Eat the food. When you get home, you'll eat like a king."

"Am I being a brat?"

"Sorta."

"Sorry. I'm just dying to see the final product. You know I'm not a patient man."

"You waited for me."

"Yeah, and that was too long, too." He snickered. "And I have to wait for you again. I need to get home."

"We need you home, too. Not long now."

"How are the horses?" he asked.

"They're doing great. They love it here."

"That's code for I'm keeping them, right?"

She laughed. "Maybe. Uh, yeah. I think so."

"As long as you're there to take care of them. I don't know shit about horses."

"You'll learn."

"I suppose. If they're nice to me."

"They'll love you."

"Promise?"

She laughed again. "You're impossible today."

"Only today?"

She cracked up. "I think you're feeling pretty good."

"I am. Except I miss you and Ollie. Love you," he said.

"Love you, too."

Dani crawled into bed, tired after a busy day. God, she missed his sarcasm and his kisses.

RICK WAS UP WHEN THE nurse entered his room.

"Today?" he asked, raising his eyebrows.

She nodded. "Yep."

His nerves kicked into high gear.

"Climb into this wheelchair and I'll take you down there."

He slipped on his robe and obeyed her. They were going to take him to the room with the mirror. He was ready. Prayers whizzed through his brain as he rode through the endless corridors of the large medical facility.

They had taken the bandages off a week earlier. He was instructed to keep his hands away from his face, to let things heal, let the swelling continue to recede and the skin return to normal. The beating of his heart was so loud, he almost didn't hear the nurse speak.

"Here we are."

"I'm ready. I think."

"Doctor Welling is waiting for you." She pushed open the door of the small examining room.

Rick left the wheelchair and sat in the seat the doctor indicated.

Dr. Welling went on and on about how the current result wasn't final, that his skin would continue to change with time, and the color would improve. He admonished Rick to stay out of the sun at all costs and to use sunblock number forty-five if he had to be exposed to the harsh rays.

The words were almost all a blur.

"I get it, Doc. Can I see now?" Rick pushed up from his chair.

"Okay. You're sure you're ready for this?"

"I've been ready for this for two years," Rick responded.

Dr. Welling handed him a hand-held mirror.

Suddenly, his heart was in his mouth, and a lump sat heavy in his stomach. Perhaps he wasn't as ready to see himself as he thought. Fear coursed through his veins along with fifty "what if" scenarios.

"Well?"

With a trembling hand and closed eyes, Rick raised the mirror. He cracked one lid open. His face was pinker than usual but smooth. His eyes flew open.

"Holy shit!"

He stared, wide-eyed at the mirror. Then turned it over and looked at the other side.

"Did you think it was a trick?" the doctor asked.

"Anything's possible. But not this. This was definitely *not* possible."

He couldn't stop staring or close his mouth.

"There's a small scar at the top of your right cheek. We couldn't remove that. Too close to your eye. It gives you character."

"My face is almost the same."

"Except for that one white scar."

"It does give me character. I can't believe Breaker Winslow is back. I can't believe you guys were able to restore my face."

"There've been a lot of new procedures in the past two years."

"I'll say. You guys specialize in miracles."

"Your face wasn't that bad."

"Yeah? Tell that to the people who hire models."

"You're exaggerating."

"Nope. My life was over."

"I don't know if this will renew your modeling career, but you should certainly succeed with the ladies."

"Only one lady I want to succeed with," Rick said before he thought.

Dr. Welling frowned for a second. "And she's worth succeeding with."

"Sorry, Doc. I forgot."

"No worries. I want Dani to be happy."

"I'll do my best."

"I'm sure you will. Let's go over what you have to do. No sun. Absolutely no sun, not now, not ever. Sunblock number forty-five. And mild soap. We don't know if your beard will grow back in those areas. Probably not."

"That's okay."

"And when shaving, be very, very careful. Especially for the first six months. Use an electric and take it slow. Let's talk about face cream and aftershave."

Rick nodded, forcing himself to listen when all he wanted to do was jump up in the air. When he finished, Dr. Welling stood up.

"You can go home."

"Thank you. Thank you a million times," Rick said extending his hand.

The doctor shook it. "You're welcome. Here's my card. Call me if you have any difficulty."

"I will. Again, I can't thank you enough." Rick couldn't stop smiling.

"Enjoy your life," Dr. Welling said and left the room.

The nurse returned. While he rode back to his room to pack up, he texted Dani.

Coming home. Face restored.

Then he called his travel agent.

"Stan? Book me on the next flight to New York. Yeah. I'm going home."

BREAKER WINSLOW WAS back big time. In the airport, he got more flirty looks from women in fifteen minutes than he'd gotten in the last two years. Oh, yes, Breaker was back. The more he studied his face, the more he realized it still wasn't good enough for modeling, although makeup would help. It had to be perfect—flawless. He couldn't get his old career back, but he could at least look in the mirror without cringing.

Taking his seat in first class, he whipped out a piece of paper. As soon as the plane was in the air, he dialed Tiffany Cowles. The least he could do for Dr. Welling was get a great interview showcasing the talents of the good doctor and his team in the paper and on television.

After he got off the phone, the woman in the seat next to him, struck up a conversation.

"Say, aren't you Breaker Winslow?"

"Sorry if my phone conversation disturbed you."

"Not at all. You are him, right? The model who had that accident."

"Guilty as charged."

"You certainly look great now," she said, blushing.

"And you are?"

"Brie Sutter, CEO of Carson and Sutter."

"The book publisher?" His eyebrows rose.

"That's right. You've been on some of our most popular books."

Now it was Rick's turn to blush. "In my prime."

"You look like you've recovered nicely," she said, giving him the once-over. "Your story might make a good book."

Before he met Dani, he'd have taken the slightly older woman up on her come-on. It was plain to him that she was angling for a date or at least a bed partner. But he wasn't playing that game anymore. With his career officially pronounced dead, he didn't need this woman. And he certainly didn't want her. He had the sweetest, sexiest woman alive waiting for him in Pine Grove. No detours needed.

Still, Brie Sutter brought him up to speed on the health of the publishing world. He sat back listening to her take on where books were headed. They shared a bottle of champagne to toast his restoration. Rick confided in her that he intended to make his relationship with Dani permanent. Ms. Sutter pouted for a moment.

"You're killing the dreams of a thousand women," she said.

"It's about time I concentrated on my own dream."

"I guess," she said, her voice dripping with disappointment.

Rick chuckled to himself. He admitted it felt good to be desired again, even if it was by someone he didn't want. What would Dani do? He prayed she'd be pleased and continue to love him.

Slightly inebriated, he left Brie and the plane and climbed into the limo scheduled to take him to Pine Grove. In the backseat, he sang along with the radio and opened the window when they crossed into Sullivan county. The fresh air made him sleepy. He dozed all the way home. He tipped the driver generously and watched him drive away. In no hurry to go inside, he wandered around back. Moonlight kissed the new fence. He headed for the barn.

Sensing a foreign presence, the horses stirred, nickering and moving about. He turned on a lantern and held it up. Their wild-eyed looks put him off. He'd scared the creatures and now a bit of his own fear backed him up against the wall. He raised his palms.

"It's okay. Really. I own the barn. You're my guests. Nothing to be afraid of."

The sound of the cocking of a gun behind him ratcheted his fear to high alert.

"Stay right there, Mister," came a familiar voice.

Holding up the lantern, he whirled around. "Dani!"

Her mouth fell open as she lowered the gun. "Rick?"

"Breaker's back!"

She continued to stare.

"What do you think?"

"I think you look...amazing."

"Much improved, eh?"

"Not that I ever had a problem with the old Rick," Dani said.

"But this one?"

"Oh my God," she uttered, placing the gun on the floor.

"Come, darling," Rick said softly.

Within a second, she was in his arms, crying and hugging him. He held her close, kissing her neck.

"Why the waterworks?" he asked.

"Happy tears."

"Me, too."

He sought her mouth for a long kiss. Then he angled his head to deepen it. The movement of the horses interrupted him. Dani stepped back.

"These are the two I was telling you about," she said, gesturing to the stalls. "Maizie is the bay, on the left, and Glory is on the right. Girls, this is Rick. The man I was telling you about."

The creatures eyed him suspiciously.

"Go over. Pet their muzzles. Speak in a soft voice. Make friends."

"It's late."

"Come on," she said, taking his hand and tugging him toward the stalls.

The horses cast nervous looks at him. He grinned and bowed before lowering his voice and approaching them. A few soft words and a gentle stroking of their noses calmed them down.

"Can we go in now?"

"What's your hurry?"

"It's been weeks and weeks since we did the deed," he whispered in her ear.

In the light from the lantern, he saw her blush.

"You have a point."

He took her hand. "Do you like my new face?"

"Of course. But I liked the old one, too."

"This is better. So much better."

"How many women tried to pick you up in the airport?"

"No one."

"Liar," she said and smiled while opening the back door to release one excited pug.

AFRAID TO APPEAR AS vain as he truly was, Rick slipped away from Dani to peek in the mirror about a hundred times a day. Was it a dream? Did he really look like that again? Only the scar on his cheek would keep him from modeling.

"Do you think you can cover this with makeup?" he asked her the next morning.

She was putting on her lipstick, preparing to go to work.

"That little thing?"

"It's not so little. If you can cover it, I might have a chance to model again."

"Here. Knock yourself out," she said, tossing a small bottle of foundation at him.

"What about the horses? Don't they have breakfast?

She tapped a piece of paper on the kitchen table. "I've written out everything you have to do here."

Rick picked up the paper. His eyebrows rose higher with every sentence.

"Holy shit! This is a lot of work."

"Not really. Oh, walk and feed Ollie, too."

"You're not taking him with you?"

"He's your dog."

"But look at him? He's standing by the door. His tail is wagging."

She kissed him. "He's yours, darling man. I could never take your place."

"Looks like you already have," he muttered, staring at the pooch.

"Jealous?"

"Definitely."

She bent down to ruffle the dog's fur. "I've got to run." She stifled a yawn.

Rick shot a salacious look at her. "Tired?"

"As if you didn't know. Keeping me up all night."

"We had to make up for lost time." He stretched his arms above his head.

"It was fantastic." She rested her palm on his chest.

Rick pulled her into his embrace. "I wish you didn't have to work. I wish you could stay. We could do the horses together. Walk Oliver. Have a life of leisure."

She cocked an eyebrow. "A life of leisure?"

He sensed his cheeks heating. "You know what I mean."

"I'm tired. Spell it out for me."

"Be together. All the time. You wouldn't have to work."

"Are you talking marriage?" Her eyes widened.

"Well, commitment. Maybe. Umm. Yeah. Maybe. Oh, okay, yeah. Maybe marriage."

"Is that a proposal?"

"Not if you don't want it to be."

Flustered and blushing, she glanced at her watch. "Oops. I'm already late. Can we talk about this another time?"

"Sure, sure. No pressure. Have a good day, sweetheart." He opened the door, planted one last kiss on her lips, and then confronted a disappointed Oliver.

"Yes, old man. You're stuck with me today." The dog barked. "I know, I know. I wish she had stayed here with us, too." He sighed. "She's gotta work. Let's go figure out what to do with those horses." He harnessed and leashed the pug, and the two headed for the barn.

When they arrived, Rick pulled down the sheet of paper pinned to the barn door. A whinny from inside told him the horses were ready to start their day.

"Ollie, it says here to either feed them first or exercise them first. But wait an hour between feeding and exercise. Hmm. How do you exercise a horse? Put on a Richard Simmons video in the barn? Maybe take them for a walk? That's possible. Harness and leash? Let's see."

Rick poked around the barn until he found the tack hanging on a hook. He took it off and turned it several ways until he found one that appeared to work.

"Isn't there supposed to be a bit with this, Ollie?" The dog barked. "Thanks. You're a big help."

He approached the bay. She stepped back in her stall. He reached out to stroke her nose. That calmed her some. He attempted to put the halter on her. She moved around and swung her head away from him. He spoke softly.

"Listen, beautiful. We have to do this thing. We have to walk. Okay? Just let me slip this on and attach that thingy, your leash, I guess, and we'll go get some exercise. Okay?"

She shot him a questioning look.

"Okay, okay. You know and I know that I don't know what I'm doing. So be kind. Okay? Give me a break."

The horse calmed enough for him to get the halter on her. It took him a minute to locate the lead. He attached it and grinned, then petted her nose.

"We're gonna get along great, Maizie."

The horse nickered. He opened the stall and led her out. She stopped halfway through the door, turning to look back at her equine companion. The chestnut in the barn whinnied.

"I'm coming for you, Glory. Honest. First, I'll get this baby out, then I'll come back for you."

The bay refused to move. Rick tried cajoling, then pushing, then pulling, but nothing worked.

"I can't take you both out at the same time. I'm only one person!" he shouted. He dropped the lead and went to get the second horse. In the meantime, the bay returned to her stall. Reaching for the second halter, Rick glanced up and saw her in her stall.

He got the halter and lead on the chestnut and tried to get her out of the barn. She also stopped at the door and looked back.

"Fuck it! I give up. Exercise time is over. Let's have breakfast."

Rick read over the instructions for feeding the horses. He did as the paper said, then added water to their troughs, pinned the paper on the barn wall and stomped out, muttering to himself.

"I smell like horse. And all for nothing. They didn't get their exercise. And I'm not grooming anyone. If they don't get out of the barn, then they lose. Dani can do it," he said to Oliver who trotted along beside him.

At the back door, he reached down to pet his dog before giving him extra treats.

"Everyone knows a pug is the only pet to have. Horses. Who needs 'em?" He shook his head and headed for the shower.

Chapter Eleven

Dani opened the door about eight thirty.

"You're late," Rick piped up.

"A bitch of a day," she said, sinking down on the sofa.

"Bad day?"

"The worst."

"Lose anyone?"

She nodded. "I don't want to talk about it."

"How about a shoulder massage?" he asked.

"Oh, God, yes."

"And a drink?"

"Vodka."

"Tonic?"

"Okay, but light on the tonic and heavy on the vodka."

"Got it," he said, moving toward the bar. After fixing drinks for both of them, he joined her and twisted her around so her back was to him. He closed his large hands over her shoulders.

"God, you're tight."

"How are the horses?" She took a sip.

"Bad news."

She stiffened. "What did you do?"

"It's okay. Really. Calm down. I fed 'em okay, but they wouldn't come out for exercise. I'm leaving that for you."

She chuckled. "Give you a hard time?"

"Damn right. Pains in the ass, if you ask me. I'll take Oliver every time."

She laughed. "Okay. I'll take them. You come with and I'll show you how it's done. They like to go out to the paddock together."

"Paddock? That's what you call it?"

She nodded.

"Good. I can stop calling it 'the field.'"

"You'll get it, Rick. Then you'll see how much fun horses are. They're really smart."

"Sure, sure. I'm happy with Oliver."

"Any food around?"

"I made dinner. Rigatoni in meat sauce. Salad. Good?"

"Oh my God, I think I love you. I'm starved." She pushed to her feet and headed for the kitchen.

As he ladled the sauce over the pasta, Dani told him the saga of the horses losing their home.

"You'll see. You'll fall in love with them. This is delicious."

"Thanks. It's not bad. Not bad," he said.

After dinner, they took the horses for a once-around the paddock, Rick walking and Dani riding. They got the animals settled, then snuggled together in bed. Dani fell asleep before his cell rang. No name came up on the screen. He eased away from his lover and padded downstairs to take the call.

"Breaker, darling!"

"Who's this?"

Fake laughter sounded from the other end. "Don't tell me you've forgotten your agent, Belinda, so fast."

"Belinda? Belinda Morgan? I haven't spoken to you in two years."

"Right, right. Because there was nothing I could do for you. But I've gotten two calls. One from *Behind the News* and one from Tiffany Cowles, herself, from *Celebs 'R Us.*"

"Really? About me?"

"Yes. They heard you'd had surgery and want to interview you."

"That's not funny, Belinda."

"It's real. I guess some paparazzi sold a picture of you to Tiffany and people said it was a fake. But he proved it was real. You've had your face fixed?"

"It wasn't broken. I had it, I guess you could say, restored."

"Oh my God. Then you're back to being the most handsome man on Earth?"

"Not exactly. But it's much improved."

"Will you do the interviews?"

"Why not? Good publicity for the miracle doctors who did the job."

"Good. I'll set up dates and call you."

"Thanks."

"By the way, welcome back."

She hung up before he could tell her he still wasn't camera fodder. He didn't care. His life in Pine Grove was full and modeling was the farthest thing from his mind. But he'd go out of his way to do a good deed for Dr. Wellington and his crew. Why not?

Not yet back in the routine, Rick remembered he owed the pug one more trip outside. He slipped the harness and leash on Oliver and headed for the last walk of the day. Thoughts about the interviews swirled in his brain. He'd have to buy some city clothes. He couldn't show up for national television in his country duds, could he? He grinned. The idea tickled him. The famous Breaker Winslow in work jeans and a flannel shirt. No one would believe it was really him. Besides, he'd had a hankering for an Italian suit tailored to his frame.

Since he lost most of his clothes in the fire, he hadn't bothered to replace much. The ones from the cleaners didn't fit anymore since he'd put on a few pounds.

The insurance would pay and he'd beg and plead with his tailor for a rush job. He hesitated, searching his mind for the name. How could he forget Federico? The man had been dressing Breaker for ten years. This would mean a trip back to the city. Perfect timing—he could check on the progress of his townhouse.

Rick slipped back into bed without waking Dani. Too bad, he could hardly wait to tell her of his good fortune. *Think of the publicity for Dr. Welling and his team.* She'd be pleased. Happy thoughts coursed through his brain as he waited for sleep to take him.

DANI LEANED DOWN TO kiss him through the open window of the limousine. Her brow furrowed, and a frown drew the corners of her mouth down.

"Don't worry. Everything's good."

"We'll see," she said taking a step back. "Safe trip."

"I'll be back in a couple of days."

She nodded as the driver put the car in gear and eased out of the driveway. Rick settled back. His mind raced. He had so many things to do in a few days. Federico had created a pattern he'd alter after measuring Rick.

As the car drew closer to the city, his anxiety intensified. Sure, he looked better, a whole lot better—normal, in fact. Except for that cheek scar. But did he still have the drop-dead gorgeous looks from his past? He doubted it. Not that he'd even considered modeling again, but how would he look on television during the interviews? Makeup was a wonderful thing. He rubbed his cheek, baby-butt smooth from his careful shave. Would he ever have that sexy scruff women wanted?

With a slight shake of his head, he remembered that he had the best woman in the world and was not in need of another. There couldn't be another woman like Dr. Dani Henderson. A smile brightened his face. He'd won her, and when he looked bad, too. It wasn't his looks, although she tended to go on a bit about his body. His grin turned to a snicker. She was one hot chick.

As he neared the city, his stomach clenched. His confidence of days past had flown. Maybe Breaker Winslow was truly dead, leaving only insecure Rick in his wake. He tried to muster the swagger of his alter ego. Breaker had assumed every woman wanted to sleep with him and every man wanted to be him, which wasn't far from the truth. He'd played the part of a celebrity, Mr. Cool, with ease. It fit him like one of Federico's custom suits. But what about now?

His first stop was the townhouse. Instead of modern, he had wanted to go country. Jess Lennox had given him some good ideas for his living quarters. He'd occupy three floors, like before and rent out the top two. This time he had a heavy-duty sprinkler system installed. He'd called up the editor of *Country Living Magazine* to get a couple of decorators' names.

The spanking new building with clean stone and a shining wrought iron banister greeted him. He smiled and tipped the driver with a one-hundred-dollar bill. Rick stood in front for a moment, fishing in his pocket for the keys Chelsea had sent him.

When he opened the door, he smelled the fresh scent of newly cut wood and recently waxed floors. Ceramic tile covered the entryway floor, and an antique combination table, mirror, and coat hook to one side. For a second, Rick didn't recognize his image in the mirror. He grinned, dispelling some of the questions in his mind. He looked great in a teal and black checked shirt and jeans.

He dropped his bag, then inspected each room. Chelsea Wall, the decorator he had hired, had done a beautiful job. His home radiated warmth and invitation. After the den, on the left when he entered, came the bedroom in the back. Muted colors, gingham and small prints graced pillows, shades, and the bed. Oh, the bed—a four-poster! He leapt on it, relishing the firm mattress and the luxurious comforter. One tall, white-washed dresser was a mate to a desk, in the corner.

He stopped in the bathroom, then the back-entrance mud room, then the kitchen. The long, granite counter and spanking new appliances called to him. He opened the refrigerator, pleased to find it stocked with beer, wine, and sandwiches.

Rick ambled back to the living room, sank down on the generous, down-filled sofa cushions, toed off his shoes, and rested his feet on the antique wood coffee table. The place had turned out better than he'd hoped. There was no doubt he'd be comfortable here, during his brief stay. What about in the future? Could he move back and live there? Why not?

Returning to the kitchen, he opened a beer and rummaged around until he found a corned beef sandwich. No one made corned beef like the famous New York delis. He took his food to the living room and turned on the television. While he ate, he caught up on local city news.

When he finished, he headed for Federico's. Time to get his new suit fitted. When he realized he'd deleted all his old friends' numbers from his phone, his spirits fell. There was no one to break bread with that night. To be honest with himself, he had to admit that even if the numbers hadn't been erased, there wasn't anyone he wanted to see. The old "gang" had deserted him in a heartbeat. Then it hit him that the only person he wanted to dine with was miles away—Dr. Dani.

TUESDAY MORNING, RICK took his new suit, shirt, and tie, still in the bag from Federico's, and hailed a cab to take him to the studio. His face got him admitted to the front desk right away, although he still had to show a driver's license. In the elevator, he wondered what Diane DiRossi was going to be like. She'd be interviewing him. Had he lost his charm? Could he take over and direct things, like he used to? Would he need to? She had no reason to be hostile. He reminded himself that this interview was about the doctors and the miracle they had performed on him.

In the suit bag was an envelope with before and after shots of him. Years ago, he'd have been too vain to show the before pictures. Now, he didn't care. He'd accepted his disfigurement as much as he could, with the help of the folks in Pine Grove. Today, he was a new man, standing tall. He took pride in his journey from a self-absorbed asshole into a man.

The minute he got off the elevator, an assistant was there to take charge of him. She gushed a greeting and ushered him into Ms. DiRossi's office.

"Nice to meet you, Mr. Winslow," the newswoman said, rising from her chair.

"Call me Rick," he said, accepting her hand.

"But aren't we interviewing Breaker?"

"Oh, yes. Forgot. Sorry."

"You assumed another identity after you were injured?"

"Sort of. My first name is Richard. Breaker is my middle name. It was my modeling name."

"I see. Welcome. Thanks for doing this. It's brave for a man like you, a model, to come on national television. I appreciate it. Have a seat. Can I get you something? Glass of wine? Water?"

"Water would be great, thank you."

Diane buzzed, and the little assistant scurried into the room, took an order from her boss, and hustled out again. She was back within seconds, handing Rick a bottle of water.

"Let's go over the interview. I don't like my guests to memorize their responses, but no one needs to go into it blind, either."

"That's perfect."

The assistant took him to the green room where he changed. Makeup artists swarmed over him as soon as he was decent. He sat in the chair as women fussed with his tie and combed his hair, then sprayed it. He'd forgotten how obnoxious hairspray was and held his breath for a few seconds until it dissipated.

In the past, when the crew came in to spruce him up, his adrenaline would kick in. He'd get wound up and let the energy flow, but not this time. It was as if several annoying flies buzzed around him. The urge to swat them grew strong. Rick pushed up from the chair and glanced in the mirror.

"Fine!" He held up his palm. "I look fine. Thank you. It's good. We're done."

One young woman brushed a small piece of lint off his arm. Rick stepped back. The young woman shrugged and headed for the door with the rest.

"Five minutes, Mr. Winslow," a young man, leaning in the door, called.

Rick raised his palm and nodded. *Did I like that shit? All the fussing? So annoying. What is wrong with me?*

Before he could answer, he was taken to the wings and within seconds, he heard his name announced, and he was onstage.

In a half hour, the lights were switched off and Rick stood shaking hands with Diane DiRossi. The interview had gone well. She had asked some tough questions that made him re-examine his motives and goals. He didn't mind. She went out of her way to make him a hero. Who wouldn't enjoy that? He gathered his pictures and personal items and entered the limo, sent by the show to return him to his townhouse. He packed up quickly, including the remaining sandwiches, as his ride back to Pine Grove was due in half an hour.

He showered, changed back into jeans, and climbed into the limo for the ride back to the tiny community he called home. As soon as they hit Sullivan County, traffic thinned. He opened the window. He opened the food bag and took out a hero before offering one to his driver, something Breaker Winslow would never have done.

He munched as he watched farms, farmhouses, and barns go by. He'd missed the scenery and the air, but most of all he'd missed Dani. Would she take his proposal seriously? His brows knit as he contemplated all the responses he could get. The only acceptable one would be "yes".

It was dark when he arrived at the farmhouse. Rick tipped the driver and eased the door open. In his bed in the living room, the snoring pug didn't take kindly to being roused, until he realized it was his master. Rick scooped up Ollie and, with his suitcase in the other hand, tiptoed up the stairs to the bedroom.

He laid the pug on the end of the bed and undressed. As he padded barefoot across the room to join his sleeping lover, the light suddenly came on and he was looking down the barrel of a Glock 9MM.

"Watch it, mister!"

"Dani!"

"Rick?" She shaded her eyes.

"Put that away."

She put the gun in the nightstand drawer.

"You almost shot me."

"I wouldn't have. When you're away, I sleep with it under my pillow."

"Can't you shoot yourself in the head that way?"

She laughed. "No way. Don't worry. You're back?"

"And shaking like a leaf. Geez. This is the second time you've pulled a gun on me."

"I have to protect myself."

"But not against me."

"Not against, you."

Her eyes shone brightly in the lamplight. He pulled down the covers and slid in next to her.

"I missed you," he said.

"Did you? Even with all those big city women and the interviews? I bet they made a big fuss over you?"

He couldn't hide his embarrassment. "So what? It's you I missed."

"I missed you, too."

Before he could reply, Oliver circled at the bottom of the bed, plopped down, and was snoring in an instant.

"Really? Show me," his voice lowered. He cupped her cheek with one hand.

Dani snuggled closer and kissed him. She swung her leg over his, pulling them belly-to-belly.

"Take me to the moon," she whispered.

"My pleasure," he said, before lowering his mouth to hers.

"POPCORN'S READY," DANI said.

"Coming." Rick carried a metal tub filled with beer and ice. Mindy and Drew, Cal, Nancy's friend from the feed store, and Nancy were coming over to watch Rick's interview with Diane DiRossi. This was his first attempt at entertaining. He served cheese and crackers, popcorn, and chips and dip with wine and beer to wash it down.

Afterward, Rick planned to cook burgers and hot dogs. Since he still wasn't over his fear of fire, he'd recruited Drew to handle the dreaded grill. Dampness under his arms signaled a rise in nerves.

"Napkins?" he asked.

"Check," Dani replied.

"Dip?"

"Check."

"Did the coleslaw arrive?"

"Nancy's bringing it."

"Potato salad?"

"Mindy and Drew."

Rick let out a breath. "That's everything then, right?"

Dani squeezed his forearm. "Don't worry. Everything's under control. It'll be fine."

"I know it's only a few people, but still. I want it to be right."

"You're gonna be a great host."

"Love you," he said, brushing her lips with his.

The doorbell interrupted them. Rick showed the guests in while Dani suggested seating. Rick noticed she had saved an empty spot for Cal next to Nancy. He smiled at her obvious attempt to get Cal together with Nancy. Why are people in love so interested in making sure the rest of the world is in love, too? He laughed to himself. Her matchmaking simply made her more adorable.

Once they were seated and everyone had drinks, Rick turned on his gigantic flat screen television. Not used to seeing himself there anymore, a jolt ran through him when he first appeared.

His family and friends applauded when he said something intelligent and laughed when he made light of his disfigurement or cracked a joke. His heart swelled to be among these people, now his people. The Italian suit fit him like a glove. Rick silently thanked Federico for an amazing last-minute job. Breaker Winslow looked fantastic.

He had moved with ease, that facility had come after many years in front of cameras. Surprised at how naturally he'd fallen back into model mode, Rick smiled. He didn't make a fool of himself and that had been his greatest worry. When the show ended, his breathing returned to normal.

"Wow, Rick. You were great," Mindy said.

"Didn't know you were so damn famous," Cal remarked.

Drew just slapped him on the shoulder. "When do we eat?"

Rick laughed and headed for the grill. He'd done his thing, paid back the doctors, and that was the end of his fame. A touch of sadness and nostalgia swept over him. He felt a slight sting of tears behind his eyes. Was that all the fame there would ever be for him?

"Medium rare, buddy," Drew said, breaking into Rick's thoughts.

"Oh, no. You're manning the grill, Drew."

Drew put an arm around his shoulders. "You can handle it."

"Nope." Rick shook his head.

"It's about time you faced it. Fire is too much a part of life to avoid it forever. You can do it," Dani said, taking his hand.

Rick threw her a questioning glance. She nodded. Rick took a few steps toward the hated grill.

"As I said before. Medium rare," Drew piped up.

"You'll eat whatever I give you."

"Of course. But if one should happen to be medium rare, I wouldn't object."

Rick turned his attention to the barbecue. Dani lit it for him. He loaded burgers and dogs on. Manning the long-necked utensils, he stood away from the heat.

"Hot dog, too?" Rick asked.

"Of course. I'm an equal opportunity eater," Drew quipped.

"Of course, you are."

"On your dollar? Anytime." The twinkle in Drew's eye brought a smile to Rick's lips. Drew was the closest he'd ever gotten to a brother.

"Can I ask you some a few things? While you cook, I mean," Nancy said.

"Sure. Fire away."

"When did you start modeling?"

Rick replied to each question, keeping his attention on the burgers, the fire, and her at the same time. Dani shot him a dirty look. He turned his head and saw Cal nursing a beer, sitting by himself.

"Psst. Nancy. See Cal over there? He's all alone. Why don't you keep him company?"

"He's fine. You and Dr. Dani just can't leave a girl alone, can you?" She shook her head but ambled over to the railing where Cal stood.

"Thank God you stopped monopolizing her," Dani said, coming up behind him, snaking her arms around his waist.

"Me? It wasn't me. She wanted to know my life history."

"I suppose. At least she's over there now."

"Jealous?" he ventured.

"Of Nancy? I don't think so."

"Pretty cocky, aren't you?"

"I'm not worried about anyone in Pine Grove. It's just everyone else in the rest of the world that bothers me," she responded.

He leaned over and kissed her. "You have nothing to worry about. No competition for you. You're in a league by yourself."

When the food was ready, they sat down at the table on the deck. Oliver curled up nearby to snatch up anything that fell on the floor. When Rick's phone rang, Dani, who had finished eating, jumped up to cut up the watermelon.

He threw a questioning look at her. She shrugged. Who could be calling him? None of his old acquaintances had his number anymore.

"Go ahead," she said.

He picked up the phone and his beer and ambled into the den to take the call.

"Rick? It's Belinda. Your interview was pure genius.

"What?"

"You heard me. My phone has been ringing off the hook. Well, maybe just one call. But it was a biggie."

"What does that have to do with me?"

"The whole world saw your interview. And I've got a job for you. An amazing job. Chance of a lifetime."

"For Breaker Winslow?"

"Yep. They called right after the interview was over. You're gonna love it."

Rick sank down on the loveseat. "Go ahead. I'm listening."

Chapter Twelve

"This guy, Don Mayer, head of marketing for Northern Brands, called me. They are coming out with a new tequila, called *Falcon*. They've been kicking around a lot of themes, then came up with pirates."

"Pirates? Isn't that image sewn up with that rum?"

"I thought so. Apparently, they don't. They have money. Bucks. Big bucks."

"And where do I fit in?"

"They are looking for a man to be *Captain Falcon*. They want pictures of him in full pirate costume, with a Falcon on his arm. When they saw you on TV, with the scar on your cheek. They said you'd be perfect."

"Me?"

"Yes. Your face is practically perfect. They said that scar makes you look like a pirate."

Rick laughed. "You're joking?" He took a sip of beer.

"I don't joke when someone mentions three million dollars."

Covering his mouth with his hand, he narrowly missed spitting beer all over the room.

"Three million dollars? Are you for real?"

"And that's just for the first year."

"First year?"

"They're planning a five-year campaign."

"Oh my God."

"My words exactly."

"There are tons of models out there. Why me?"

"You're already high profile. Your interview was huge. And you're on a million book covers."

"Not anymore," he said.

"Those covers never die."

"You're not shitting me?"

"It's absolutely true. I'll send you the contract when we agree on the deal."

"The deal?"

"Salary, travel expenses, payment schedule, that stuff. The boring stuff that you never wanted to know about."

"Oh, yeah. That stuff," he said.

"Is it a go?"

"Are you kidding? Of course."

"Good. I'll start ironing out the details on Monday. Have a good weekend, Rick. I'll be in touch. Or should I say 'Breaker'?"

"Breaker?"

"You're back, baby. Back and bigger and better than ever."

"Thanks for this, Belinda."

"Don't thank me. It's your face that did the trick. Oh, by the way, if you're still shaving your chest, stop. They want a pirate with an open shirt and a hairy chest."

"I stopped doing that after the fire."

"Great! We don't have to wait for it to grow in to start shooting."

"Please don't agree to a schedule without checking with me first."

"Why? You've got something else going on?"

"Actually, I do."

"Work?"

"Just check with me."

"Oh, I get it. A girl. Okay. Will do. I'll be in touch. Oh, and thanks, Rick. You've just paid for my kid's college." She hung up.

Dani poked her nose in. "Everything okay?

"I've got a job. I think. Maybe."

"A job?" She joined him on the loveseat.

"It's complicated. I'll tell you after dinner."

"Okay. Is this good news or bad?" Her brow furrowed.

"Good. I think."

"Okay, then," she said, pecking him on the cheek. "Come back to the table."

"Don't say anything to anyone, okay?"

She smiled and nodded.

What did this mean? Would he get his old life back, too? Happiness mixed with confusion in his heart. He sat quietly, listening with only half an ear to the conversation. Rick attempted to smile and nod at appropriate times. Was he Breaker again? Would that beast raise his handsome head from the ashes, like a phoenix? Did he want that? Hadn't a return to his former life been the constant prayer on his lips for the past two years?

He volunteered to do the dishes after dinner. The quiet in the kitchen gave him time to think. Mindy wandered in. She picked up a stray carrot stick and chewed.

"So, Cuz, what's up with you? Are you feeling all right?"

"I'm fine." No way could he discuss this with her.

"What happened to Mr. Life-of-the-Party? After you left to take that call, you clammed up. Something wrong?"

"Fine. Everything's fine."

She pulled on his arm. "No, it isn't."

Facing her, he made eye contact. Mindy was the one person who'd always loved him. He had blown bubbles with her, taken her joyriding in his new car, flirted with her girlfriends, and bought her luxurious Christmas gifts. She'd been the one to pick up the pieces, what was left of him, after the fire. He couldn't hide the truth from her.

"It's complicated."

"Bullshit."

He shifted his weight. "Okay. I've got a job. Modeling."

"Really? Fantastic!"

"Is it?"

"Of course. I want to hear all about it."

"I can't talk until the contract is signed."

"Oh. Okay."

He dropped his gaze to his hands. The secret burned inside him, dying to get out. Mindy's advice had always been reliable. Besides, she was the only one he truly trusted, except Dani.

"You want to tell me, don't you?"

He nodded, still not raising his eyes to hers.

"I'll stop. It's okay. You'll tell me when you can. I hope it brings good things to you, Rick. You deserve a break."

"I have Oliver and Dani. That's luck enough."

She laughed. "I've never heard you talk like that. The sky's the limit. Bring it on. Success breeds success. I've got a million clichés that tripped out of your mouth."

"That was then and this is now. Go on. You're spoiling the party. People will wonder what's going on. And I've got dishes to finish."

Mindy left the room. Rick picked up the sponge and vowed not to think about Captain Falcon Tequila anymore. No sense making himself crazy when nothing was even signed. There'd be plenty of time to worry after this became official. Now, it was a fifteen-million-dollar pipe dream. Or at least that's what he told himself.

"ARE YOU COMING TO BED?" Dani asked as she stood in the kitchen doorway?

Rick sat on the deck holding a glass of brandy with Oliver by his side.

"Not yet. I'll be up soon. Just want to finish this."

She sauntered outside. "Something's bugging you. Are you going to tell me or make me guess? Is it about this mysterious job?"

"Come on. Sit down. You have a right to know."

He related everything Belinda had told him.

"You have to wait until sometime on Monday to know if this is going through?"

"That's right."

"And if it does, what does that mean?"

He took a breath, glanced at his drink, and then finished it. "It means I might be traveling a bit. Prepping for photo shoots, appearing at events."

"You'll be playing the role of Captain Falcon?"

"Yep."

"Can you wear those clothes in bed?"

He cocked an eyebrow at her, then burst out laughing. Rick closed his arms around her and pulled her close. "Leave it to you to find the humor."

"I don't see the problem. I mean if you're just going to be putting on silly clothes and standing in front of a camera for a couple of days and getting paid a ton—what's wrong with that."

"It's much more than that."

She cocked an eyebrow.

"I'll be shooting television commercials, too. Might have to go on location."

"Okay, so one trip."

"It might be a wee bit more intrusive than that," he said and hoped she stopped asking questions.

"Let's go to bed." She reached for his hand.

He kissed her head, then pushed to his feet. "The magic words."

In bed, he leaned back from her for a moment.

"Is it better with me looking like this?"

"You're a great lover. A few scars never made a difference to me."

"Good."

"Why?"

"Just want to know if the looks really matter."

"Not to me."

"Didn't think so. Nice to have that confirmed."

"Enough talking. Your woman is horny," she whispered in his ear.

"Hell. Let's do something about that," he said, bending to kiss her shoulder.

The next day, they hung around the house. Dani taught Rick to ride the bay, they ate leftovers and made love. The horses accepted him, sort of. He laughed at their antics and marveled at their strength and beauty. Wearing only fluffy robes, Rick and Dani dined on cold ham and potato salad on the deck. He watched the horses graze. An early chill in the air reminded him that summer was about over. Next weekend was Labor Day.

He pushed Captain Falcon out of his mind, but fall was in the air and that meant Christmas promotions would be underway in another month. He figured liquor companies promoted big for the holidays. Concentrating on Dani's chatter proved challenging when all he could think about was Falcon Tequila. Being wanted again whetted his previously dormant appetite for fame. The sweet taste of revenge against those who said he was finished filled him. Their words came back.

"Looks aren't everything."

"Well, there are other careers outside of modeling."

"Shit happens. I've got an audition. Gotta run."

"It was time you moved over and let someone else have a little limelight, anyway."

"Aren't you getting a bit old for modeling?"

Old, he'd been thirty-one at the time. Coming back had been his greatest dream, one he'd thought he'd never achieve. Now, he had his chance, maybe, and he could hardly breathe, as he waited to find out.

"You're not listening," Dani said.

"I'm sorry. I can't seem to stop thinking about Captain Falcon."

She simply nodded. "I get it."

"Do you? I don't think anyone who hasn't been in my place really could. My entire career went up in smoke." He chuckled. "Seriously. It was gone in a second, a moment, through no fault of mine. Unless trying to rescue my dog is a weakness. It was ripped away. I wasn't ready to give it up."

"And now?"

"Now? I don't know." He shrugged.

"At least that's honest."

"There's a lot riding on this."

"The money?" She raised her eyebrows.

"Yes and no. The chance to be back on top. To be wanted, to be sought after. You can't imagine the high that brings."

"Since I'm not wanted, no, I can't imagine." She pushed to her feet.

"Hey, don't do that. Come on. Don't take offense. You know what I mean."

"Oh, yes, I do. Definitely, I do."

"I want you. And Pine Grove wants you." He tugged on her hand.

"I suppose."

"Fame is an incredible jolt, high, whatever you want to call it."

She sat back down next to him. "And what about us, if you become Captain Falcon?"

"Us? You're the best thing that's ever happened to me, Dani." He moved his chair closer and bent to kiss her. The doorbell rang.

He completed the kiss and muttered all the way to the front of the house, "Who the hell is coming by now?"

Retying his robe, he grasped the knob.

"Special delivery," the man in the uniform said. He held out a thick envelope.

Rick took it and signed on the dotted line.

"Thank you, sir."

Rick nodded and backed up.

"Say, aren't you Breaker Winslow?"

"I am."

"Can I have your autograph?"

"Sure."

Rick scrawled his John Hancock on the paper the man offered, then returned inside. It almost always felt good to get a request for an autograph, except when his girl was waiting. He slid his hand under the flap and peeked inside as he returned to the deck.

"What's that?"

He shrugged, pulling out an official looking document. He picked up his phone and dialed.

"Belinda? What's this you sent me?"

"The contract for Captain Falcon. I looked it over. It's good. No worries. Sign it and return it to me ASAP."

"Not before my lawyer looks at it."

"You have a lawyer out there in the boonies?"

"Of course I have a lawyer."

"I need it back right away. They want to start shooting by the end of next week."

"Christ! Really?"

"Yes. Get this done and get it back to me. It's time to rock and roll. Breaker Winslow lives." She hung up.

Stunned, he looked up at Dani. "And so it begins."

MINDY AND DREW STOPPED by the farmhouse. Drew, Rick's lawyer, carried a manila envelope under his arm.

They sat in the kitchen while Rick made a cup of coffee. Dani was at the clinic.

"I went over this and had the Falcon Tequila lawyer make some changes. He faxed me the revised contract. It's okay for you to sign." Drew pulled a pen out of his breast pocket.

Rick thumbed through to the last page and added his signature.

"Can you send it back for me? I don't have any courier service out here."

"Sure. No problem." Drew put the contract back in the envelope.

"Jess made some chicken salad for us for lunch," Rick said, heading for the fridge.

Mindy helped him pull the meal together and raised her mug. "To the rebirth of Breaker Winslow."

They clinked their coffees and drank.

"Is this a good thing?" Drew asked. "I mean the money is phenomenal. But the work and the fame, all over again?"

"I've been wondering about that, too. I'm not sure," Rick said.

"It's a lot to take in, I'm sure," Mindy said.

"I was certain this would never happen again. And things here are going well. But I can't turn this down, it's too big. And I have a score to settle," Rick said.

"With who?"

"With myself."

After they left, he cleaned up and headed upstairs to pack. Oliver padded after his master. Rick opened his closet and frowned. In the townhouse, he'd had a closet the size of a small bedroom. His wardrobe had consisted of everything from the most expensive jeans to several tuxedos in slightly different styles.

Living in Pine Grove, he hadn't bothered to recreate the extensive selection of suits, shirts, and pants. He hadn't needed anything more than T-shirts, flannel shirts, and jeans. He picked up the phone and called Federico. While the company would provide the costume for him to wear during the shoot, he needed some tony leisure clothes.

"Federico, please," Rick said. "Ah, my friend. I am coming back to New York. Yes. And I need some casual clothes. Can I make a list and text it to you? Perfect. Thank you."

How easily he slipped back into the mode of rich, famous man and being waited on. He'd always been a comfort lover, but after leaving that behind for two years, he was surprised how easy it was to go back to that lifestyle. In Pine Grove, Rick had had to fend for himself. The old Breaker Winslow would never feed hay to a horse—he'd have hired someone to do the task. Rick looked forward to being with the mares. He talked to them while he gave them breakfast. Cooking, cleaning, doing dishes—all tasks Breaker Winslow would never do. And the chicken barbecues, garage sales, and especially the kissing booth, would never have had the pleasure of Breaker Winslow's company.

While picking out a few items to bring to New York, he peered at himself in the mirror. He looked like the old Breaker Winslow, but was he? There was something about him, something different—maybe his eyes? The cool blue had turned warm. He grinned. The smile appeared genuine, not forced or fake. He'd practiced in front of the mirror every day before he had hit it big. His carefully invented cool expression had become second nature back then—now it was gone.

He needed to focus on his future and holding onto Dani through the turmoil that would become his life. He mustn't let her slip away. He reminded himself that she was the only real thing, the only one who truly cared. Except for Mindy, his cousin, who didn't count.

He laid his garments in the suitcase, then headed downstairs. After clipping the harness and leash on Oliver, they walked the grounds. He looked around, memorizing every twig and blade of grass. This was his spread, freedom, and happiness awaited him here. After he'd gone out to conquer the world, he'd return to his kingdom, horses, pup, and woman.

At six he flipped open a cookbook to a super salad recipe and started dinner. He turned the radio on to his favorite local station and hummed along as he chopped, sliced, and diced his way into greens heaven. Cooking his last meal for Dani until who knew when, he grew nostalgic. Dani and Oliver made great dinner partners. He didn't know when he'd be back. Everything depended on how well the shoot went and what other commitments Falcon Tequila had for him. He fed Oliver then dressed the salad. Dani would be home any time.

The atmosphere at dinner was stiff. Dani seemed on the verge of tears. She didn't have much appetite. Rick's heart clenched. He wished he could say something to ease her worries. But he didn't know what lay ahead any more than she did. He'd been down this road before. Who knew if he had the power to keep his head straight through this shit shower? Though he'd try, he wouldn't bank on it. When she pushed her plate away, he took her hand and kissed it.

"I have your favorite, Panda Paws, for dessert."

She shook her head.

"Turning down ice cream? You must be sick."

She tried to smile but didn't quite accomplish it. "Maybe just a small bowl?"

"You got it."

After dinner, they went right to bed. After making love, she cried. Her tears stabbed his heart. He held her until exhaustion brought a quick end to snuggling. They were asleep by ten.

Rick awoke at five. He showered and dressed quietly, then finished packing. He took Ollie out before making breakfast. He left two pancakes for Dani. The limousine was due at seven.

Rick crawled up on the bed and kissed a sleepy Dani awake.

"Sweetheart. I'm leaving in a few minutes."

"Oh, okay," she replied.

He kissed her until she kept her eyes open.

"You awake? I'm ready to go. The limo will be here any minute."

She clung to him. "I wish you weren't leaving. I know that's selfish."

"I'll be back, darling," he said, stroking her hair.

"Will you?" She looked up at him. "I wish I could believe that."

"Believe it. You're one of a kind, Dani Henderson. Don't forget that."

"Will you be safe among all those wolves?"

"I used to be one of them."

"But you're not now."

"I can handle them," he said with all the confidence he could muster.

"I hope so."

A horn honked twice. It was time to go. He kissed her with everything he had, then slid from her embrace and headed downstairs. Yawning, Oliver followed. At the door, Rick picked up the dog. He snuggled his face into the pug's side.

"Be good, Ollie. Watch over Dani. I'll be back boy. I love you."

And in a flash, he was out the door, into the vehicle, and on his way back through the gates of Hell.

Chapter Thirteen

At six o'clock the next morning, Belinda texted him a schedule for the week. At nine, he was to meet the executives at Falcon Tequila. He silently praised the tailor when he donned his newest suit from Federico, and his thousand-dollar shoes, and eight-hundred-dollar Kobey tie.

He had a limousine at his disposal during the period when he would be shooting. He texted the number and, in fifteen minutes, the town car pulled up in front of his house on the corner of 77th Street and West End Avenue. Falcon Tequila, a division of Northern Brands, had offices in the fifteen floors the parent company occupied at 55th Street & Avenue of the Americas.

Don Mayer, head of marketing, met Rick in the lobby and escorted him upstairs. Rick spent the next three hours viewing a slide presentation on the launch of new product and meeting with the top executives of both Falcon Tequila and Northern Brands.

The men stressed the necessity that the product launch be perfect. They reiterated why he was selected.

"You were the unanimous choice of the executive committee, Breaker," Don Mayer said.

"Thank you."

Rick turned on the charm. Like riding a bike, it came back to him in a heartbeat. He cracked jokes and told some salacious stories about his adventures as the most sought-after male model in the U.S. for five years. He had the execs eating out of his hand by lunchtime.

They took him to The Palm, one of the priciest steakhouses in the City. Rick had a seafood salad. While the executives had two cocktails each, Rick drank one ginger ale. He had to watch his weight. Alcohol was fattening and lowered inhibitions. Rick didn't want to say anything that would threaten the deal.

Pleased he'd built a rapport with the men who'd hired him, Rick hopped in the limo and headed for the studio. An attractive, tall redhead greeted him.

"Hi, I'm Vanessa, account supervisor on the Falcon Tequila account. You can call me Van, everyone does," she said, sticking out her hand.

"Nice to meet you," he said, meeting her firm grip.

Her eyes breezed over his form and a small smile crept across her face.

Whoa! If she thinks I'm going to have sex with her while we do this, she's mistaken.

In the past, the look she gave him would have had him salivating. He had had affairs with most of the female ad agency staff as well as the female photographers and assistants he'd come across in his career. It had almost become standard operating procedure. One sexy smile from him and the millennial chicks would melt on the floor.

"I've heard all about you," Van said, her eyes glowing.

"I don't know what you've heard, but I'm engaged to be married, and a faithful fiancé."

Her expression changed. "Thanks for telling me," she said, her tone cool.

"Where's wardrobe?"

"Right this way. Olga is here to do the fitting."

He wasn't really engaged. Dani hadn't said yes yet, but he figured that to be simply a technicality. She loved him, he loved her—marriage was the next step.

He turned the corner, and standing in the dressing room, straightened up to her full four-foot-eleven inches stood Madame Olga. Rick remembered her from a zillion past shoots.

"Olga!" He greeted her with a hug that swept her off her feet.

"Put me down, you Casanova!" The tiny woman, not a day under seventy, pounded his biceps.

He laughed as he returned her gently to the floor.

"You bad boy. How are you? I heard all about you. But look at you now? You look better than ever."

"Flattery will get you everywhere, Miss Olga."

"You dog. How have you been?"

They spent a few minutes catching up.

"Okay, strip down to your skivvies, mister," she commanded with her hands on her hips.

He did as he was told. She pulled out a measuring tape.

"Colleen! Come in here!" Olga called.

A pretty young woman, not much over nineteen, entered the room. She had bouncy, brown curly hair to her shoulders and big blue eyes.

Totally comfortable being undressed in front of people, Rick didn't turn a hair, until he looked at Olga's assistant. She blushed to the roots of her hair. He laughed.

"Think of me as wearing a bathing suit and we're on the beach."

Olga patted his back. "Perfect."

"Take this down," the older woman commanded.

She measured him from head to toe. Colleen kept her gaze on her notebook, her blush slowly abating. After the measurements, Van turned him over to the photographer, Mala, and her assistant. They had him doing different poses so she could light him and make notes.

"We will be shooting inside and out. We'll take a few shots today for measurement of light and evaluation of you," Mala said.

He glanced at her hand and noticed a wedding band. He sighed, relieved to find a woman who would not be sizing him up for her bed.

The afternoon was spent holding various poses while Mala shot. It was a tiring day. They brought in lunch and continued to work through the afternoon. Olga had her seamstresses working on his costumes before they finished lunch. At five o'clock, Olga told him they'd be ready for fittings in two days.

"We will evaluate the shots tomorrow morning and set the schedule for the location shots," Mala said, shaking his hand.

"Is the location schedule set up yet?" he asked Mala.

"Talk to Van. The Agency is handling that. Good work, Breaker. The camera loves you. I expect this shoot to go very well."

"Thank you."

Her positive attitude buoyed his spirits. In the men's room, he wiped sweaty hands on a towel. Until Mala had said something, he had no idea if he'd still be photogenic enough to keep this assignment. Slowly his confidence returned. At six thirty, the limo drove him back to his townhouse. He poured a stiff vodka tonic and sat by the window.

He found a fat envelope in the mail. It was the full production schedule for the ad campaign for Falcon Tequila. With closing dates for November and December magazines looming in the near future, the next three weeks were packed. There were to be stills shot on location as well as in the studio.

Then there were three television commercials to be filmed and aired throughout the holiday season. There were two locations for the television commercials. He'd be flying to the Caribbean, then to Florida.

Wardrobe fittings were scheduled for the next two days, then studio shots for three days, then on the road for three weeks. Peaceful days contemplating life disappeared. His stomach knotted at the prospect of all the togetherness with the agency people and the dirty old men from Falcon Tequila. His life had become quiet, tranquil, and countrified. He'd have to readjust to the fast track and quickly.

He sighed and dialed Dani. The phone went directly to voicemail. He checked his watch. She was still working. He left a message, ordered in Chinese food and took a shower. He was in bed asleep by nine and didn't even hear the phone ring.

Early in the morning, he awoke to Dani's message. Were they going to be communicating only by voicemail? Were their schedules so out of synch that he'd never speak directly to her?

He brewed coffee, then sat and watched the birds in his backyard. Hadn't he prayed for his old life back? Wasn't this what he'd wanted? He stared outside, searching his heart for the answer. The one phrase that kept recycling through his brain was, "Be careful what you wish for."

DANI TOOK OVER RICK'S closet. Not that she had a ton of clothes. What does a veterinarian need with more than one little black dress and several pairs of jeans? She had to live in his house to take care of the horses. Besides, Oliver was more comfortable in his own home. A little piece of Dani assumed that if she was living in his house, he couldn't walk away from her easily. At least she hoped that was true.

Nancy came over once a week to break bread. Mindy and Drew checked in on her, too. While she maintained she'd lived alone for a long time and didn't need anyone watching over her, she did welcome the company.

Texts came from Rick almost nightly. He called when he had the chance. Often, she was at the clinic, embroiled in an emergency or with a full schedule of exams and neutering. The inability to coordinate their schedules frustrated the hell out of her. She longed to speak to him directly. News stories, especially on the Internet, showed him in groups of people, often surrounded by sexy young women.

Although she tried to slough those off as mere publicity, doubt about his fidelity crept into her heart. Always independent, Dani marveled at how much she missed him and how essential he'd become to her wellbeing. One night at three a.m., unable to sleep, she padded down to the kitchen. Between sips of milk, she received a text from Rick.

Hope you're okay. I'm good. I've been lying to the people here and the media. Have to tell you, in case you see it.

Dani's stomach hit the floor. Her mouth got dry and her heartbeat thumped loudly in her ear. She licked her lips. Did she want to know? Probably not.

What did you tell them?

Her hand shook when the phone dinged with his reply.

I told them I was engaged to you. I know you didn't say yes. I know it's not true. Doesn't mean you can't back out. Are you mad?

Tears of relief rolled down her cheeks. Mad? No way.

I could kiss you right now. That's awesome. Betting if you actually asked me, the answer would be 'yes'.

She downed the rest of her milk and headed for the bedroom.

It's late. Couldn't sleep. Worried you'd see that and dump me. Yawning. Going back to bed. Love you.

She climbed into bed and pulled up the covers before texting her reply.

Love you, too.

Oliver trotted along behind her. He jumped up and did his circles before settling down. He gave her an annoyed look, yawned, and closed his eyes.

"Right, boy. Sorry to wake you. Rick's okay. I'm okay. We're okay. Nothing for you to worry about."

She settled into the bed, snuggling into her pillow and pretending it was her lover. After a big sigh, she grinned and let sleep overtake her.

A phone call woke her at six. A dog had been poisoned. She threw on clothes and raced out the door with Oliver tucked under her arm.

It was just the beginning of a busy day. She had surgeries, neutering, exams to give, and a horse with a possible case of colic to call on. On the go all day, at lunchtime, she returned to Rick's to feed the horses.

After several apologies she wasn't sure the mares were buying, she fed them and gave them fresh water. Fortunately, Rick had left her money to hire someone to muck out the stalls. She had had her fill of dirty jobs with the animals at the clinic and farm animals. She didn't need more at the barn.

Taking a small break, she sat on a stool while the ladies chowed down. She checked her phone and found several early morning texts from Rick. He was in the Caribbean and phone service was spotty. All five texts arrived at once.

Leaning against the door, she read each one. She kept up with his adventures. How exciting to be the center of attention for a major photo shoot and commercial. Perhaps the product, Falcon Tequila, was the true center of attention, but Rick was right there along with the bottle. What about female attention? Dani never questioned that there was plenty of that to go around.

He'd sent a photo of himself in full pirate costume, his shirt opened to the waist, his chest called to her. God, he looked gorgeous. So sexy with his eye patch, scar, which they had emphasized with makeup, and that salacious grin. She sighed, feeling stirrings below she hadn't noticed in a while. She wanted to lock him in the bedroom for days. Perhaps he was already getting all the bed bouncing he needed?

One picture he'd attached showed him in a tavern, surrounded by sexy women wearing off-the-shoulder, revealing costumes. How many of those women had thrown themselves at Rick? Probably all of them. Her spirits fell. A whinny from the bay brought her attention back to the mares.

"I don't know if he's coming back, girls. We'd best find you a new home as soon as possible."

The chestnut stomped her foot in protest. Dani shrugged, called to Oliver, and headed back to the clinic. She'd received many dinner invitations from the folks of Pine Grove. They took care of their own. They didn't want Dr. Dani breaking bread alone. But she didn't have the heart to socialize. At the end of her overstuffed days, she was too tired to drag herself out of the house.

Doubt dogged her steps as she went through her day, forcing thoughts of Rick out of her mind. Forgetting about Rick got a tad easier as pictures and headlines of shenanigans in the Caribbean danced before her eyes. Loneliness didn't appear to be a problem for him.

Life had seemed so simple before Rick left. The only way to recapture that would be to forget Rick Winslow completely. Dani was working on it.

"COME ON, BREAKER. DON'T be a party pooper." A young woman tugged on his sleeve. "We're going to the Buccaneer. You gotta come, too."

It was eight, and he was hungry. The twelve-hour day was finally over. He wanted a shower, a stiff drink, and a huge plate of food. Besides the woman was far too young for him. He eyed her coldly.

"Go on without me, Natalia," he said and backed away.

"But you're the life of the party. You're such a fun guy." She shot him a flirtatious look.

Three years ago, he'd have had a bet with himself at how long it would take to get her into bed. Now, all he wanted was to be alone, eat dinner, and fall into bed—alone.

"Come on, Breaker. One drink. One little ole drink. The ladies love you," Tom, the account executive said.

"You going?" Rick cocked an eyebrow.

"Are you kidding? With all these hot women?"

Rick saw the gleam in the agency man's eyes and recognized it. Three years ago, it would have appeared in Rick's eyes, too.

"One drink. That's all. Do they have food there?"

"Yep. Come on," Tom said, taking Rick's arm.

"Breaker's coming! Yay!" Natalia cheered.

"You can have her, I'll take Beth," Tom whispered in Rick's ear.

He stiffened. "I'll take whoever I want and you can have the leftovers. That is, if I want anyone at all."

Tom laughed. "You telling me you'd walk away from this prime beef?"

"That's exactly what I'm telling you."

"Then you're a fool. And I'd never have taken Breaker Winslow for a fool."

They pushed three tables together and quickly filled them with production assistants, models, and agency people. Beautiful young women flanked Rick. He ordered a burger and vodka tonic. While Tom made his feeble and obvious attempt to pick up a couple of the women, Rick chowed down. He enjoyed watching Tom pull some tired, old moves.

Chuckling to himself, he remembered the best move of all. He'd look for the vainest chick in the group and then purposely ignore her. It didn't take long for her to decide to seduce him. Damn, it worked every time. He contemplated telling this to Tom but discarded the idea. Let the poor jerk fend for himself.

One more week in St. Thomas, then back to New York for more fittings, and some grueling days at the studio. After he ate, he ordered another drink then slipped out of the restaurant. He heard the soft lapping of the waves and made his way to the beach. Strolling and drinking, he stared at the moon, then out to sea.

Questions circled his brain. Where did he belong? He fit back into the fast crowd seamlessly—as if he'd never left. While that life wasn't the Eden he'd remembered, it wasn't the worst place in the world, either. Luxury flowed everywhere—limousines, fabulously expensive meals, the best liquor, and lavish hotels created enchantment. Hell, it sure beat mucking out a stall in his barn. He laughed out loud.

In the past week, he'd had calls from old *friends* who had deserted him immediately following the fire. Astonished at the rapidity of their desertion, he'd howled and bled over their callousness and lack of loyalty. Now they had returned, attempting to worm their way back into his good graces. He chuckled at the word *worm*, for surely that was apt.

The flattery of attention from top talent agents, decorators, and wealthy real estate tycoons almost seduced him. Although certain he had his head on straight—Rick was confused. How could something that looked so good be so bad?

Party invitations flooded in via text. And the temptation to attend them all, just to show off and shoot them the bird burned in his chest. The memories of the smell of fine leather sofas, the taste of the most expensive caviar, and smoothness of the finest liquor assaulted his mind. Important people hanging on his every word had seduced him before. Not anymore. Breaker Winslow, reborn, literally, from the ashes was a different man. No longer a shallow fellow, no longer a party animal, he'd become grittier, tougher, colder, and a helluva lot more discerning. Still, the lure of returning to have the last goodbye to the false friends that filled his former life called to him, and he lacked the power to resist.

Should he give them one more chance? He opened his phone. There was the invite from Channing Laurelton, President and CEO of Talent Unlimited, to a party at the posh Starlight Room of the tony Silver Spoon Hotel on Park Avenue. Breaker was to be the guest of honor. Laurelton's wife, Phoebe, was president of the ad agency that held the Falcon Tequila account. He couldn't miss that party, could he?

He texted *accept* to the invitation and grinned. Work would be finished. This was the elegant "wrap" party. And it would be his party, his night, in every way. He finished his drink and started back to the hotel.

Catching a glimpse of Tom trying to talk one of the young women into coming back to his room, Rick stopped.

"Rebecca!" he called.

She and Tom turned. Rick jogged a few steps to catch up to them. He offered Rebecca his arm.

"It's very late. You should be asleep. Shall I escort you home?"

"Oh, Breaker. Yes." She sighed and took his arm.

Ignoring the cold stare from Tom, Rick showed the woman to her room.

"Won't you come in?" she asked.

"My dear, you're too young, too drunk, and too pretty. And I'm an old engaged man. Goodnight."

He closed the door on the surprised female and headed back to his room. Too late to call Dani. He simply texted her, *I love you,* then went to bed.

DANI WALKED INTO THE clinic early on Monday. Nancy was already there. She wore her glasses low on her nose and peered over them at the doctor.

"Looks like we might have a taker for the horses. And your boyfriend is sure tomcatting around the Big Apple these days."

"What do you mean?" Dani came up behind her friend and peered at the computer screen.

Breaker's back!

Breaker Winslow, the famous model who lost his looks in a fire has come back like a phoenix, or is it Frankenstein's monster? After extensive plastic surgery, Winslow has retaken his crown as king of sexy ads as the new image for Falcon Tequila.

After a hectic shoot in the Caribbean and the coast of Florida, Breaker breaks out with a night at the tony nightclub, The Backyard.

The picture showed Breaker dancing with two girls wearing skimpy outfits. He was grinning. Young men and women, crammed into a small room appeared happy and drunk. Dani stepped away.

"It's his life, Nancy."

"Yep. Just sayin'..."

"I get it."

She went into her office and closed the door. Sinking into her chair, her heart racing, she took two deep breaths. Then the phone rang. Her heart leapt up. *Rick?*

Disappointment stung her when she saw Mindy Winslow's name on the display.

"Hi, Mindy." She tried to sound enthusiastic.

"Did you see Rick on the Internet today?"

"Yep."

"Look, don't worry. I know he's not fooling around with those girls."

"How do you know?"

"I just know. He's not into that anymore. He has you."

"This way he can have his cake and eat it, too," Dani said, even though she knew that he couldn't have her if he was sleeping around.

"Please, please don't judge him. When did you last speak to him?"

She shrugged. "Do you consider exchanging texts speaking?"

"I mean actually talked to him."

"Don't remember."

Silence followed.

"Crap," Mindy said.

"Have you spoken to him?"

"Twice since he got to New York."

"And?"

"And he was not into the whole scene. He doesn't want to go back to the life he had."

"Could've fooled me."

"Please, Dani?"

She blew out a breath. "Okay. I won't make any decisions until I speak to him again."

"Decisions?"

"There aren't really any decisions to make, are there?"

"Well..."

"I mean when he comes back. If he comes back. The decision will be his, won't it?"

"You'll have a say, too."

"Will I?"

"Of course," Mindy said.

"We'll see. I gotta go. Patients. Thanks for calling."

"Can you come to dinner tomorrow night?"

"I've been working pretty late. I'm not much company these days."

"Please. We'll wait dinner for you."

"Okay. I'll stop by after work."

"Great! Take care, Dani. Don't give up on Rick."

"See you tomorrow."

She hung up. She wasn't giving up on him, perhaps it was the other way around?

Nancy buzzed from the front desk.

"I have three possibles for the mares. Do you want to interview them?"

"Could you set it up for next week?"

"Sure thing."

The sooner she placed them, the quicker she could move out of Rick's place. Living there had gone from delightful to painful in the two months he'd been gone. His presence was everywhere, but he wasn't there. She sighed, picked up her stethoscope and headed for the lobby. She had work to do and couldn't waste time mooning over the famous Breaker Winslow.

She didn't get to her lunch break until three.

"Letter for you," Nancy said, handing over an envelope.

Dani looked at the return address. It was from some lawyer in New York. She opened it and out fell a check. She picked it up. After reading the amount her eyebrows shot up.

"What is it?" Nancy got up from her desk and came around to take a look. Dani handed the check to her.

"It's for the horses."

"Is there a letter?" The receptionist asked.

Nodding, Dani unfolded the paper. She read it aloud.

Dear Dr. Henderson,

On behalf of Richard B. Winslow, I enclose a check in the amount of ten thousand dollars for the purchase of the two horses currently living

in

his barn. He will be in touch with you for further instructions.

Sincerely,

Robert Allberg

"Rick's buying the horses?" Nancy asked.

"I guess so. Check's made out to the clinic," Dani replied.

"Wow. That's a chunk of change."

Dani smiled. "He's making a donation."

"Damn generous, if you ask me."

Dani smiled and handed the check to Nancy.

"Guess I can cancel those interviews for the mares?"

Dani went into her office and unwrapped her sandwich. Was Rick being generous or was this his way of keeping her in his house until he got back? Either way, she had to admire his craftiness. Even though he seemed up to his armpits in sexy women, he had taken the time to ensure she'd be there waiting for him. She shook her head. *Breaker is back, oh, yes, he is.*

Chapter Fourteen

Wrap parties usually didn't require black tie. They were often wild affairs, but not this one. He'd learned to tie his tuxedo tie years ago. He brushed his thick hair back and stared at his face. Rick had made friends with the little white scar that wouldn't go away. He'd decided it gave him class, made him distinctive, rugged, even. And the Falcon Tequila folks loved it.

He looked forward to margaritas. They probably wouldn't serve anything but tequila. He didn't mind. Several of his former friends had called him to tell him they were going to the party. He didn't give a rat's ass if they showed or not. And the three old girlfriends, all former models, called, angling to be his date for the party. He enjoyed turning them down like they had turned a cold shoulder to him when he needed a place to stay after the fire.

That was how he got to Pine Grove. His cousin Mindy took him in when all his rich *buddies and bed buddies* ignored him. The tables were turned, and he'd enjoy watching them grovel to get back in his good graces. There wasn't anything they could do, no depth they could sink to that would reinstate them with Rick. Although he had to thank them—going to Pine Grove had been the best move of his life.

The limo picked him up at seven on the dot. He sat back and looked out the window. The sidewalks were crowded with people rushing to get home from work, others heading to restaurants. They were the pulse of the city. The energy permeated his body, speeding up his heart rate slightly. The city confused him. He had a new life now, but the rhythm of the city still awakened his drive, sparked his creativity. It had become part of him and always would be. He sighed and tried to sort out his feelings as the car wove in and out of traffic to get to Park Avenue.

He dialed Dani, but it went to voicemail. A glance at his watch told him she wouldn't be off work yet. A dose of Dr. Dani Henderson was what he needed to keep his head on straight. His brow furrowed. What would he find as he passed through the gates of Hell, back into his old life?

The car stopped, and a doorman opened the door. Rick smoothed his jacket down and pushed to his feet. The crisp autumn air sent a slight chill through him. Or was it due to the impending disaster of a party?

The elevator whisked him to the top floor. When he stepped out, there were balloons everywhere and pirate decorations. Posters of him holding a bottle of Falcon Tequila were splashed across the walls. When he spied the crowd of people in formal attire in the large ballroom, he sucked in a deep breath before entering.

Don Mayer rushed over to greet him.

"Breaker! So glad you're here. Come. I want you to meet some people." The marketing man threw one arm around Rick's back and propelled him through the thickening crowd. His eye was drawn to long brunette hair cascading down a naked back. Curiosity about how much of the front was actually covered drew his attention.

"Oh, yes. Melody Parker. Says she knows you," Don said, stopping.

The woman turned around. Wide straps barely covering her breasts joined together behind her neck.

"Well, hello, Breaker. Long time," she said, reaching up to kiss his cheek.

He'd bedded her at least a dozen times, yet couldn't conjure up the feel of her skin or the warmth of her kiss. The statuesque beauty radiated a cold sexuality, a look-but-don't-touch sensation in him. He had no passion for her, she aroused nothing in him.

"Long time," he said, nodding before turning away to head farther into the room. A slight coolness on his cheek where she'd kissed him reminded him of why they didn't last. Suddenly, he was starving.

"Where can I get some food?" he asked Don.

"Right this way. Open bar, too." They threaded their way through the throng of sycophants and brown-nosers who hailed him as he passed. Some called out their names to refresh his memory, some made quick allusions to a previous connection with him. He nodded and smiled as needed.

"Only margaritas tonight. What's your poison?" the bartender asked.

Rick ordered a strawberry margarita and eyed the buffet table. His stomach rumbled. He needed to eat, to avoid getting drunk. In this group, being drunk would guarantee him starting a scene with some-one, any of a dozen or so people who professed to be his best friend or his most prized lover. No way could he handle this crap on an empty stomach.

"Food," he muttered, putting his drink down and grabbing an emp-ty plate. He filled it with hot and cold hors d'oeuvres and chowed down. As he was chewing the top brass from Falcon surrounded him.

"Breaker, my boy! Great shots."

"Amazing commercial!"

"Early audience tests are off the charts."

"This is going to be the best ad campaign ever."

He made eye contact but continued to stuff his face with shrimp, melted brie on toast, fried zucchini sticks, and cheese. He downed his drink, keeping eye contact with the men chattering away at him. The treasurer took him aside.

"Here's the copy of your check we sent to your agent. We've also made that donation to the charity you mentioned. Here's the proof." He handed Rick an envelope, which he inserted in his breast pocket.

"Thank you. That means a lot to me."

"We're predicting a big success for this. That means there will be a phase two."

"Phase two?"

"Didn't your agent tell you? If this campaign sells tequila, we will be launching a second campaign in time for summer. And you'll be the star again."

"Oh. Great." Rick tried to summon enthusiasm for Falcon Tequila's plans but didn't quite succeed.

"I'm sure you're tired and would like to spend a week or two in the Bahamas," the president said. "Looks like there are a few ladies here who would like to go with you."

Rick's gaze scanned the faces and cringed inside. There wasn't anyone there he'd want to spend even one day with, let alone two weeks. Oh, no, Dani, only Dani would accompany him anywhere he went.

"I'm engaged, in case you didn't know," Rick put in.

"Really?" The man's eyebrows shot up. "Maybe we can make it an all tequila wedding? That would be something, wouldn't it? And we'd pay for everything."

The idea of turning his wedding into a sideshow to sell tequila turned his stomach.

"I've monopolized too much of your time already. Just wanted to thank you for a job well done. We look forward to working with you again." The man shook his hand and wandered off toward the bar.

"Breaker, darling! Where have you been?" a female voice cooed in his ear.

He spun to face his last girlfriend before the fire, Jasmine Taylor, model-turned-actress.

DANI TOOK TWO HOURS for lunch and went shopping for the horses. She needed blankets, nicer halters, and a few other things. She didn't buy the cheapest items. With Rick's ten grand she'd get better quality gear that would look nice and last longer.

She'd had some missed calls from him and a few voicemails, but they were few and far between. Maybe the new life was catching up to him? She bit a nail. Would he come home to her or fall for the lure of the glamorous world of fame?

Dani paid for her purchases, arranged to have them delivered, then headed back to the clinic.

"Any emergencies while I was out?"

"Nope. Not a one," Nancy said, looking up from her paperwork.

Dani gave a half-smile and retreated to her office.

"You've got no excuse to work late tonight," the receptionist said, following her boss.

"What difference does it make if I work late or not?"

"Go home early. Call Rick. You're a mess."

"I'm not a mess. I'm just fine with him gone."

Nancy laughed. "No matter how you dress it, a polecat is still a polecat. Fool yourself, you're not fooling me. You need him. You need to find out what's going on and when he's coming home."

"You mean *if*, don't you?"

"I mean *when*. I always say what I mean." Nancy frowned before turning on her heel.

Dani sat back and rested her feet on the trash can. Every week there were more questions about Rick. Three weeks had easily become six. Cool winds foreshadowed the arrival of winter. Questions she texted to him came back with vague answers or no response at all. The picture came more and more into focus as time went on. His new life had seduced Rick. Return dates kept getting pushed back. First, it was reshooting, then the wrap party, and now there were interviews around the campaign launch and appearances at major retailers.

Another solo Thanksgiving loomed ahead, like a monster, threatening to engulf her. Last year, an emergency saved the day. The owner of a sick horse had called her away from her turkey sandwich and canned cranberries. The family was so grateful, they set a place for her at their table.

Hoping for a miracle to save the holiday didn't seem like a viable plan. She'd have to make her own luck. That's it! She'd have her own Thanksgiving! She'd invite Nancy, Cal, the guy at the feed store, and the pharmacist and his wife. Five people. That would be just enough for her to handle. Of course, she'd set a place for Rick, but she doubted he'd show.

Nine that night, Dani sat down with leftovers, a glass of wine, and a pad and pen. She started to make her holiday feast shopping list. As she glanced around the room, envy invaded her chest. How wonderful to be able to cook a magnificent Thanksgiving dinner in this kitchen. It was practically a professional one, with all the trappings, including a chef's refrigerator and stove. Images of sharing a bottle of red wine on a frosty November day while padding around the room, peeking into pots, chopping things on the counter—and with Rick.

Her phone rang. It was him.

"You're in?"

"Yep."

"How are you? My God, I miss you, Dani. So, so much."

"Do you?"

"Don't you believe me?"

"It would be easier to believe if I heard from you occasionally. And if you told me when you're coming home."

Silence.

"It's not that simple. I signed on for a lot more than Belinda told me. Openings in major cities, interviews. Christ, all kinds of shit. Believe me, I'd rather be at home with you than here in Chicago. It's damn cold."

"So, come home, then," she said, her eyes filling.

"As soon as I can."

Tears streamed down her cheeks. She grabbed a tissue and dabbed at her face. Struggling to control her emotions, she took a deep breath before speaking.

"Did you hear me, Dani? Are we still connected?"

That was the big question.

"I'm here. I'm here."

"Yeah. You're there and I'm here. What's wrong with this picture? Could you come out

here? Take a little time off?"

She shook her head. "Not possible. I have a sick horse I'm looking after. And there's Will Lennox's dog, Laura's cat. Spays, neuters, Mr. Kress's cows. It's never-ending."

"Isn't there a back-up person?"

"Nope. The former vet is too sick, and they haven't found a replacement back-up yet."

"That's because you're doing the job of two. Why don't you kick back a little?"

"Why don't you?" Anger tinged her tone.

"I'm on contract."

"So am I. The contract I have with the people of Pine Grove to look after their animals."

"The sick horse isn't one of our mares, is it?"

At the word "ours" her heart clenched.

"No," she squeaked out.

"Thank God. Your work is more important. Trust me. I get that. Doesn't make me miss you any less."

"It's late."

"I get the hint. Okay. I love you. Sleep well, pretty lady."

"You, too," she said, cutting their connection before a sob broke from her throat.

Oliver pushed up from his bed to settle on the floor by her side. Dani hid her face in her hands as sobs tore from her. Her shoulders shook a wee bit and her tears wetted the table. She still loved Rick. While it warmed her heart, it also made her mad. And there was still one, unanswered question in her mind, *will he ever come home?*

NOVEMBER FIRST, RICK woke up with a hangover. Halloween had been totally insane. The party had started behind the scenes. The ad agency folks had brought in a case of champagne to celebrate the new campaign launch. Rick guessed it was doing well.

Sitting in his pirate costume, getting made up, he had the sipped champagne. It wasn't Moet & Chandon, but he'd settled. The sipping had become a second glass, then a third. By the time he had to appear in Times Square, he was already floating.

Falcon Tequila had rounded up two hundred people by offering free coupons and free candy. In addition, they'd hired over a hundred actors to flesh out the crowd. Breaker had stood on the dais with the broadcasters. He had waved, struck pirate poses, and laughed with the people.

The more people had to drink, the rowdier the crowd became. Then the event had taken a turn on the wild side right before midnight. Many of the young people there were high on something and police had to step in. There had been an after-party in the Falcon Tequila suite at the Americana Hotel overlooking Broadway. Jasmine Taylor had been there and had made a play for Rick.

"Stay with me, Breaker," she whispered in his ear, slipping her arm around his waist.

"I don't think so." He disengaged her and headed for the bar. "Ginger ale, please."

"Come on. For old times' sake?"

He shook his head and took a big sip.

"You're no fun."

"Just a stuffy old engaged man."

"You're not married yet. What's one more fling?"

He laughed. "Not gonna happen. Sink your claws into someone else."

"You don't have to be rude." She frowned, turning hostile eyes on him.

"Don't mean to be. But you've got to learn to take *no* for an answer."

"Men don't turn me down."

"I'm the exception."

"Have another drink. Maybe I can change your mind."

He laughed again, then pushed through the crowd looking for the door. On his way, Don Mayer buttonholed him. Drinks kept appearing in his hand and, fool that he had been, he had downed them. At three in the morning, he had staggered to his hotel suite, ripped off his stupid costume and passed out in bed.

The next thing he knew, he had a monumental headache, and something was chiming in his ear. Cracking open one eye, he spied his phone. Dani. He picked it up and croaked out a greeting.

"Rick?"

Before he could respond, a female voice piped up.

"Shut that fucking thing off."

Rick's eyes flew open, and he turned to face the other person in the bed. Jasmine Taylor, naked, with a sheet mostly wrapped around her, stared at him with bloodshot eyes.

"Who's that?" It was Dani.

Rick put his hand over Jasmine's mouth. She squirmed, so he moved back, thrust his legs over the side, and, grimacing, pushed to his feet. He retreated to the bathroom and shut the door.

"Dani?"

"I heard a woman. Who was that?"

"I must have left the television on."

"Don't lie to me. They don't use the eff word."

"They do on cable."

"Come on, Rick. If you have a woman there, you'd better tell me now, before I read about it in the papers."

He hung his head. "I don't know how Jasmine got in here."

"That's a good one. Try again."

"I'm telling the truth. I stayed at the Halloween party until three. Got totally hammered and passed out here, in my room, in bed, alone."

"Then how'd she get there?"

"I don't have a clue. Honest. Believe me. I'll ask her and call you back."

"Gives you plenty of time to get it right. Don't rush calling me back. I'm very busy," Dani said, before ending the call.

"Shit." Rick stared at the phone before grabbing a towel. He fastened it around his waist then opened the door. "Jasmine, what the fuck are you doing here?"

"I couldn't go back to my hotel."

"How'd you get in?"

"The hotel manager was nice enough to give me your room number and your key. He knew all about us."

"Asshole," Rick muttered. "You've gotta go." He sank down on a chair opposite the bed. Jasmine threw off the covers.

"Sure you don't want any of this?"

He had to admit to himself she looked damn good.

"Nope. I told you. I'm engaged."

An evil look came into her eyes. "Really? Even after that phone conversation? Sure she's still your girl?"

He gulped. She had a point. Dani was pissed, and Rick didn't know how to fix it. He was innocent, but no one would believe it. Hell, if he'd been in her shoes, he wouldn't have believed it either.

"You have to leave. Now."

"Now?" She arched an eyebrow.

"That's what I said. Now." Hell, he was only human, and he'd been without a warm, female body way too long.

"How about one for old times' sake, Breaker?"

"Out. Now!" He rose from his chair and scooped up her discarded clothing. He tossed it on the bed. "Get dressed."

She rose slowly, wiggling whatever would jiggle and sending him flirtatious glances. It would be so easy to have a quickie with her, relieve himself, and reduce his stress and tension. After all, who would know? Just Rick and Jasmine, right?

His old life called to him, luring him to partake, simply taste what it was like to sleep with Jasmine, drink too much, and live much of his life hungover. Had he been an alcoholic? He figured he hadn't, but he'd come damn close. As for women—they were at his beck-and-call all hours of the day and night. Not hookers, top women—models, journalists, actresses, politicians, you name it, he'd slept with them all.

Sure, Jasmine wouldn't blab to the papers, but Rick would know. He'd know he'd broken his commitment to Dani. He couldn't do it, no matter how horny and tempted he was.

"Get dressed." *Before I change my mind.*

"You're such an old man, Breaker. You used to be fun. Up for anything," she said, then giggled. "Up for anything. Get it?

"Yeah, yeah. I got it. Hurry up, Jasmine. Before the press gets wind of this."

"Of what? Nothing happened."

"You and I know that, but no one else'll believe it. Especially not *Celebs 'R Us.*"

She shrugged. "I don't give a damn. Might do my career some good."

He cocked an eyebrow. "Your career? You in trouble?"

"Not really. Just a few slow months." She stepped into her skintight black satin pants.

"I'm sure things'll pick up." He trained his gaze out the window. Sometimes watching a woman get dressed was as sexy as watching her disrobe. But that was if he'd slept with her.

She fastened the snug red vest around her ample breasts and picked up her jacket.

"It's been great, Breaker."

"What's been great?"

"Seeing you. Spending the night together."

"We didn't."

"Oh, but we did. Maybe nothing happened, but we slept in the same bed together."

"Hell, I didn't even know you were there!"

She grinned. "Just yanking your chain, sweetheart. For old times' sake."

He gave a weak smile. "Forget it. This never happened."

"Fine. Whatever." She made a dismissive gesture with her hand. "See you around. If you change your mind, you know where to reach me."

He had no clue where to reach her and that was fine with him. She shrugged her coat on and tossed him a dazzling smile.

"You look great. The surgery was a success. Good luck, Breaker. Keep in touch." With that, she was out the door.

His head throbbed. He picked up the phone, ordered room service, including ibuprofen and a gallon of water. He dragged himself to the closet and selected a pair of jeans and a T-shirt.

The way he felt, he didn't know up from down. He rubbed his scratchy face. Was bringing him back to this world a good idea or bad? He searched for the answer with the part of his mind that still functioned when there was a knock on the door.

Chapter Fifteen

Anger burned in Dani's chest as she placed her phone on the desk in her office. Rick had spent the night with a woman. A model, probably. What was the likelihood that he didn't sleep with her? Probably zero—after all, it had been months since she and Rick had made love. He was not a man to give up sex for long periods of time.

She sighed. It had finally happened. The tenuous thread that had held them together had broken. Their connection had given way to the temptation of a luscious, willing model. Dani was done, finished, gone, through, kaput—walking away, as far away as she could get from Rick Winslow, the two-timing bastard.

With eyes blazing, she headed for the front desk.

"Nancy, where's the number for that horse-boarding place?"

"Give me a minute," the receptionist said, shuffling through her Rolodex. "What's up?"

"Nothing. I'm done babysitting Rick Winslow's horses. We'll move them to the boarding place, then I'm moving out of his house."

"You are?"

"Damn right."

"Here's the number."

"Good. Please call them and say we want to move the horses right away. Today."

"You're sure this is what you want to do?"

"Damn right, I'm sure. Should have done it months ago. There's enough money to pay for them."

"They won't get as good care as they'd get from you," Nancy pointed out.

Dani stopped and sucked in her lower lip. Nancy was right. No one could care for the mares like she had. She always added a big dose of TLC along with the hay and the grooming.

"They'll be okay," Dani replied.

"Maybe. But just okay. How do you think they'll like it?"

Dani shifted her weight and glanced at the ground.

"Call 'em," Dani said, turning on her heel. "Who's next?"

"Mr. Walters is here with his cat. She's due to get shots."

"Okay, then. Let's go. Mr. Walters, please come this way." The doctor led him back to the examination rooms.

At the end of the day, Dani washed her hands and joined Nancy for a cup of tea.

"So, did you get the horses moved?"

The receptionist shook her head. "They're all full up until after Thanksgiving."

"After Thanksgiving?" Dani almost spit out her tea.

"Yep. Looks like you're gonna have to stay there a bit."

"Damn," Dani swore softly, directing her gaze out the window.

"Looks like you can still have that great Thanksgiving you were planning."

"That?"

"Yeah. That. Some of us were counting on it. I know Cal at the feed store's been talking about it for weeks."

Dani smiled. "He has?"

"Yep. I was kinda looking forward to it, too. And in that house," Nancy sighed.

"It's stunning," Dani agreed.

"Guess you can put up with it for a bit longer, then?" Nancy stifled a smile.

"Guess I'll have to. Can't leave the horses there alone."

"Nope. Can't do that. You gonna tell Rick?"

She shook her head. "I bet he's already figured it out."

Dani turned on her cell. There were twelve messages and texts from Rick. Each text was more desperate than the one before.

"Guess he hasn't figured it out yet," Nancy said, glancing over at the phone screen.

"He's one stubborn man."

"Have you listened to his side yet?"

"Sort of."

"Hmm. Conviction with no trial. That's damned unamerican."

"I suppose," Dani replied.

"Doc, you need to get the facts. You've got him executed without even listening to his side."

Dani recounted her conversation with Rick and the female voice in the background.

"He lied at first. But I caught him. Doesn't exactly do a lot for his credibility."

"Hell, I'd probably lie too, if caught up like that. Give the man a chance," Nancy said.

"He's had plenty of chances. He's not coming home, Nancy. Face it. I have. Now I need to stop taking care of the mares and living in his house."

Nancy sighed and shrugged. "After Thanksgiving, you can do whatever you want."

"Damn right I can. And I will." She stomped off, grabbed her coat, and left the clinic. Righteous indignation burned in her breast. Justification after justification streamed through her head. Searching for solace, she licked her wounds but got no relief. None of it made her feel any better. If she'd been honest with Nancy, she would have admitted that she didn't want to leave his house, his bed, or his heart. What she wanted more than anything was for him to come home to her—no more excuses, no more commercials, public appearances, or parties.

But she had no indication that would ever happen. She pouted like a little kid, wallowed in her pity party, and yearned for what she could not have.

After she made a drink, she sat down in front of the television. A text drew her attention. It was from Nancy.

Turn on Channel seventeen now!

Dani did as she was told. Tiffany Cowles appeared. Seemed like she was doing an interview. Was this with Breaker? She could care less. As she was about to switch it off, a familiar voice caught her ear. It was the woman from Rick's hotel room!

"We are so lucky to have Jasmine Taylor here today. How are you?"

"Fine, Tiffany. Thank you for having me."

"We want to hear all about your next project, but first, I understand you were discovered in Breaker Winslow's hotel room."

"That's true."

"I hear he's engaged. Is that true?"

"Yes, but..."

"Uh, uh, uh. I guess the leopard can't change his spots. Still tomcatting around, even though he's got a woman waiting for him?"

If Tiffany Cowles had plunged a knife into Dani's chest, it couldn't have hurt any more.

"No. Wait a minute. I need to set the record straight. Sure, we were at the same party. But that was all. I'd had a bit too much to drink. I got the hotel clerk to let me into Breaker's room. He'd told me he was staying there. He's an old friend and he helped me out, gave me a place to crash. I really didn't feel well. Nothing happened between us."

"Nothing?" Tiffany's eyebrows shot up.

"Nothing. The man's got it bad for some chick, and he's keepin' it in his pants."

"Well, knock me over with a feather! Breaker Winslow faithful to one woman?"

"Yep. You heard it here first."

"It's hard to believe you, Jasmine."

"Wish I was her. She's a lucky girl."

"Damn right. Rumor has it you're heading for South America to do a new indie flick..."

Dani switched off the television. Her cell rang. It was Nancy.

"Did you see that?"

"I did. I'm flabbergasted."

"Well, stuff my cabbage, the man is telling the truth!"

"Who would have thought?"

"Not you, that's for sure," Nancy said with a chuckle.

Shame filled Dani. Had she misjudged him? Maybe.

"YOU'RE WELCOME TO COME to my house, Breaker. I know my relatives would love to meet you," Don Mayer said.

"Thanks, Don. I have plans," Rick lied.

They sat in the lobby of the hotel, waiting for a limo to take them to the airport. They had two more cities to do before they broke for Thanksgiving. Jasmine Taylor sauntered up.

"Darling, come to my house. I have something to stuff that's lots more fun than a turkey," she cooed in his ear.

He laughed. "Thanks, but no."

She made a face. A man announced her name, and she caught his attention. He was a limousine driver. Jasmine waved, blew Rick a kiss, and was gone in a flash. He released a breath. Relief at her leaving eased the knot in his gut.

"I thought she'd never leave," he muttered.

"Jasmine Taylor? You've got to be kidding me. If she made a play for me, I might even be unfaithful to my wife," Don said, his eyes following the model's butt to the door.

"She's all yours."

Don shook his head. "I don't get it."

"You would if you had a woman like mine at home. No offense to your wife."

"You've got someone better than Jasmine Taylor?" Don looked at Rick.

"Damn right she's better. It's personal. Trust me. She's better."

"So, what are you doing here?"

"Fulfilling my damn contract."

Don nodded. "The offer for Thanksgiving still stands."

"Thanks."

Two vehicles pulled up. Don got in one and Rick in the other. After they hit the highway, Rick got out his phone. He called his cousin.

"Hey, how's it going? I saw the commercial. You looked great."

"Thanks. Is Drew there?"

"Just a sec."

Rick glanced out the window, watching the strange city pass by in a blur. He had visited city after city, town after town, and liquor store after liquor store. He was dizzy and couldn't even remember what state he was in.

"Rick?"

"Hey, Drew. How's that deal coming?"

"Paperwork is just about done. I'll be delivering it for her signature next week."

"Excellent. Do I need to look it over?"

"I don't think so. I believe I got all the points you mentioned."

"Humor me. Let's go over the list one more time," Rick said.

"You're the client. Go ahead," Drew responded.

The men went over Rick's list. Every point was covered. Satisfied that something in his life was going right, he thanked his cousin-in-law and hung up.

Stuck in rush hour traffic, Rick sat back against the leather seat. He hadn't been able to reach Dani for ten days. Calls and texts went unanswered. In his gut, he sensed he was losing her. Frowning, he reached into the breast pocket of his jacket and pulled out a folded piece of paper—the schedule. Tonight, he was scheduled to fly to Washington, then on to Boston, then Toronto, finishing up two days before Christmas in Buffalo.

"Buffalo?" His brows shot up. "Really? Christmas in Buffalo." His heart sank. He shook his head. He wasn't a puppet, but a human being, with a life. Finally, he had a life—didn't he? He had had one or thought he had.

His eyes watered. Dr. Dani Henderson. He needed her more every day he was away. His old life encroached, creeping closer and closer, threatening to engulf him. Would she wait for him? Since she hadn't responded, it didn't seem like she would. His heart grew heavy.

It hit him. This was same old, same old. Modeling took over and made love impossible.

"Not this time," Rick said.

"Excuse me, sir?" the driver asked.

"Nothing. Nothing. Just talking to myself."

Why hadn't he seen it before? Even if he hadn't slept with Jasmine, he'd slipped back into the old habits. Drinking too much, partying, staying up late were all reminiscent of the way things used to be before the fire. The only thing missing was sex.

He laughed to himself. This had to stop now. If he could deal with the lack of sex, he could do anything! Yes. *Time to grow up and stop letting others run your life.* Rules were made to be broken. Commitment had to come first.

He hadn't signed on for this brutal schedule. Belinda had made the plans, and, like a mouse, he'd simply gone along with everything. What did Belinda care if he lost the love of his life? She didn't give a damn. As long as she got her fifteen percent on time, nothing else mattered.

Anger steamed up in his chest. He'd been a fool, but no longer. Buffalo could go to Hell, along with Boston, Washington, and Toronto. He clenched his jaw. Breaker Winslow would step aside so Rick Winslow could have a life.

He hit speed dial on his phone.

"Belinda?"

DANI AWOKE TO FIND frost on the windows of Rick's bedroom. It was six Thanksgiving morning. She lay still, realizing it was her second to last day in this exquisite farmhouse. Tomorrow, she'd pack up. Will Lennox would arrive to transfer the horses to the boarding facility. She refused to let sadness ruin this special day. If it was to be her last curtain call, then she'd make it a grand one before returning to her mundane existence.

Oliver yawned, then burrowed farther under the covers.

"Time to get up, Ollie. Gotta get that damn turkey in the oven. Come on, boy." Dani threw the covers off and swung her feet to the floor. With a yowl, she stood, shivering, on the cold wood. After grabbing her bathrobe, she addressed the pug.

"I'm not giving you back to Rick. I don't care what he says. You've been with me a long time. I'm used to you. You're going to be my dog, not his. It's okay. You and me. Right?" She grinned as the pooch barked once, then leapt off the bed and headed downstairs. Dani caught up with him in the kitchen. Oliver sat at attention, awaiting his morning meal.

Dani fed the dog and put up a pot of coffee before returning to the bedroom to get dressed. She consulted her list and the timeline she and Nancy had put together. Mindy and Drew were joining them since the Pine Grove Playhouse, Mindy's baby, was doing a Thanksgiving evening performance and the young woman had no time to prepare a big meal.

According to her list and the clock, Dani had an hour to chill before starting preparation. She leashed Oliver, slipped an envelope under her arm and headed for the backfield. She let the dog off the leash as they approached the barn. He liked to run in and greet the horses every morning. His bark was answered by a neigh from one of the mares. As she moseyed along, Dani pulled out the contents of an envelope Drew had dropped off the day before.

First, there was a letter from Drew, then an official-looking document. She scanned the letter. The words *Henderson Animal Rescue* jumped out at her. What the hell? She read on. In the document, Drew explained that a non-profit animal rescue corporation had been formed with her as CEO. Turning to the second page, she saw that the operation was underwritten by a one- hundred-thousand-dollar grant from Falcon Tequila.

Her breath caught, her eyes watered. *Rick did this!* Thumbing through the rest of the document, her eyes glazed over at the legal mumbo-jumbo she'd have Drew explain when he arrived. Her heart sped up as emotion stuck in her throat. Rick had forced Falcon Tequila to do this, for her, just for her. Her mind raced with all the things she could do with the money, all the horses, cats, and dogs she could rescue—maybe even a few pigs!

Arriving at the barn, she greeted the girls. Her tears wouldn't stop. She hugged the bay, sharing her love and emotion. The horse stood still, supporting the doctor. She wiped the wetness from her cheeks and tried to smile. She'd miss the mares. They had become friends. Sure, the place they'd be boarding would provide a good home, but not nearly the same amount of love Dani gave. Or Rick, either, for that matter. He'd grown attached to them, too.

She chugged her coffee and took care of the animals. Blowing a stray hair out of her face, she glanced at her watch and realized it was time to get the feast underway. She whistled for Oliver, who trotted along beside her as she headed back to the house.

On the way, thoughts of rebuffing the animal rescue company swirled in her mind. Hurt by his refusal to return, Dani didn't want any gifts from him. A frown settled on her lips.

Before her huff picked up steam, ideas for things she could do with the money and the homes she could provide for homeless and abused animals ran through her mind. That kind of money would buy a lot of meals and provide shelter for so many in need. She decided there was no way she could turn away the generous gift. If she saw it as something for the animals and not for her, she'd accept it.

She shook her head. Assuming he wanted to get back with her was pretty ballsy, even for her. Dani gave a short laugh. This wasn't a *let's get back together* gift, it was more like a pay-off, a soothe-my-conscience thing. If so, fine, she'd accept it, and make the most of every penny. It was pretty obvious Rick wasn't coming back, regardless of what Jasmine Taylor thought. She sighed. She had told herself a hundred times that he wasn't, but a little part of her had still held out hope. Now that this had arrived, it had confirmed her hunch that her man had moved on.

Before she could vent her feelings, the doorbell rang. It was Nancy, right on time.

"Let's get started? Where's our list?" Nancy said, donning a spare apron. When the doctor didn't answer, she stopped to stare at Dani. "What is it?"

Dani choked on the words, so she just handed the letter to Nancy. The older woman read it quickly.

"Well, shear my sheep! How great is this? You can do so much good. Rick must've made this happen."

Dani nodded, still unable to control her voice. Her eyes watered.

"What's to be sad about? Don't you want to do this? Isn't this who you are?"

Dani took a deep breath, forcing herself to speak. "It's his farewell gift."

"Well call me a gopher! What kind of silly thing is that to say?"

"It's the truth. This is to make me feel better. He's not coming home, Nancy. Ever."

"You don't know that. Don't be a horse's ass. The man is out making a mighty fortune and you expect him to hold your hand every minute of the day. Grow a pair, lady."

"What do you mean?"

"If a man can't expect his woman to make it through tough times, then what's he got? A stupid goat, buttin' his head against a wall. Girl, you've got to be stronger than that."

"What makes you think he's coming back?"

"No man ever did something like this for a chick he planned to leave behind."

Dani stopped. "You're right, it's strange. But then, Rick isn't your ordinary guy."

"He's a thoroughbred. Don't you go being a candidate for the glue factory. You gotta have faith, girl."

Dani tried to smile.

"Come on. We got a crew comin' looking for a major meal. Time's a wastin.'"

Nancy rolled up her sleeves and washed her hands. Dani joined her.

"It says here, we start with the stuffing," Dani said, perusing the list.

"First you gotta preheat the oven, girl."

DANI AND NANCY HAD split up, heading for different rooms to take naps before people arrived. The gray day didn't get brighter. The temperature stayed a steady thirty-eight degrees. Oliver joined Dani in bed. She wrapped them both in a blanket Nancy had crocheted for her.

The house smelled wonderful. The aroma of roasting turkey filled every room with the promise of a mouth-watering meal. The table was set, the side dishes were made, and the cheese and crackers simply had to be arranged on a cutting board. She peered out the back window as she stroked Ollie.

Too busy to focus on her own life for the past few hours, her heart grew too heavy to sleep. Preparing a sumptuous meal in Rick's house that he'd never enjoy tugged on her heart. She wanted him there more than anything. But it was two-thirty, with no sign of him, so she had to let go of hope. Could Nancy possibly be right? Was the nonprofit a gesture of love, instead of a kiss-off? She'd never know unless she saw him again.

She had to own his lack of phone calls. She'd refused to talk to him after discovering a woman in his room. That had been the final straw. Closing her eyes, she dozed, relieved of her worries for an hour. The alarm went off at three-thirty. She changed clothes and headed for the kitchen to find Nancy there.

"Well, it's about time, missy!"

"I was resting."

"Good thing, too. You were as worn out as an elephant delivering twins." Nancy patted her arm.

"What do we have left?" Dani asked, picking up the list.

The ladies stocked the bar, put the hors d'oeuvres on the coffee table, and shoved the green bean casserole in the oven. At four on the dot, the doorbell rang. Cal, bearing a fresh pie, arrived first. Then Mindy and Drew came in. The pharmacist and his wife arrived shortly after.

While Nancy and Dani went back and forth from the living room to the kitchen, Drew handled the bar.

"Do you have any questions about that document I sent over?" He asked Dani.

"I haven't had a chance to go over it much yet. It's amazing. We can do so much good."

"Rick arranged that with Falcon. In case you hadn't guessed."

"I figured," she replied.

A timer went off.

"That means it's time for dinner. Into the dining room, folks," Nancy said as she ushered people to the table.

The guests took their seats. Dani lingered for a moment longer, her heart full. What if? No, no way was he coming. It was too late. She sighed, petted Oliver, who had been drooling by the oven all day, and turned toward the dining room. The click of a key in the lock drew her attention. The door burst open with a whoosh of frigid air, but Dani didn't feel cold.

"God damn traffic! I should have been here an hour ago!" Rick said, unbuttoning his coat. He stopped to stare at Dani, whose face was covered with tears.

"You're here?"

"Of course, I'm here. Where else would I be? With my girl on my favorite holiday of the year," he said opening his arms.

Dani flew into his embrace. He held her close, kissing her hair as she sobbed into his chest.

"Who left the damn door open? Raised in a barn? The turkey's gonna get cold," Nancy said barreling into the living room. She stopped, and her mouth fell open. "Rick?"

"Well, it ain't Quasimodo." He cradled Dani as she calmed down.

Within seconds, the others had joined them. Nancy shut the door.

"Leave it to my cousin to make the entrance of the year," Mindy said, shaking her head.

"Thank God. I didn't think you'd make it," Drew said, coming forward to shake Rick's hand.

"You knew he was coming?" Mindy turned to her husband.

"He asked me to keep it a secret."

Mindy gave Drew a playful slap on the arm.

Dani stepped back, and Rick brought his mouth down to hers. The passionate kiss brought applause from the onlookers and a red face from Cal.

"Where the hell is the food? I'm starving," Rick said, slinging his arm around Dani's shoulders as he strode to the dining room.

Nancy scurried into the kitchen to retrieve another place-setting.

"I can't believe you're here," Dani said, gazing up into his eyes.

"I'm here, for good."

"What about the contract?"

"Contracts are made to be amended, right, Drew?"

His cousin-in-law nodded as he tucked his napkin into his shirt.

"Amended?"

"Belinda signed that on my behalf. But she never checked with me. I wouldn't have agreed to it back then and I sure as hell don't now. With Drew's help, we changed it. In the future, I will give them two, two-week trips. That's all. The rest of the time, I'll be here, with you. If you'll have me," he said.

"You're back for good? You're staying?"

"Absolutely. We've got a rescue to run. Together. If that's okay. I mean, you're the CEO. It's all up to you."

"Are you sure this is where you want to be?"

"Never been more sure of anything in my life," he replied.

"But what about—?" He put his finger on her lips.

"Don't. I needed to get back into that life. To see it for what it is. Needed to leave it on my own. That's not for me. This is for me. You, Oliver, the girls—this is where I want to be. I want to grow old with you, Dani. Marry me," he said and slipped a small box out of his pocket.

Dani gasped when he opened it to reveal a large, marquis-cut diamond ring. She covered her mouth with her hands.

"Holy cannoli!" Nancy said, her eyes bugging out.

"Nice, Cuz," Mindy said, smiling at Rick.

"Well?"

"Yes, oh, yes. Yes, I will," Dani replied.

They turned from their seats to kiss while the spectators applauded.

"Okay. Drama and romance are over. Drew, carve the damn turkey. I'm starving," Rick said.

Oliver barked.

Rick pushed back his chair, stood, and picked up the pug. He snuggled his face into the dog's belly while the creature barked, then licked him.

"We've missed you," Dani said, passing a bowl of stuffing.

Mindy uncorked a bottle of wine and poured. The sound of knives and forks clinking together silenced the crowd. Rick returned to his seat and kissed Dani once more. His eyes watered.

"It's so good to be here," he said.

"Welcome, home," Dani replied cupping his cheek.

Epilogue

Jess Lennox's dream to renovate the enormous, deserted, old house on Route 32 by Cedar Lake had kept her going through the dark days of her father's murder and her mother's incarceration. The house overlooked the lake, though it didn't have lakefront property. She'd been in love with that old wreck for years.

She sat down, cross-legged by the back of the house to eat her peanut butter and jelly sandwich. Of course, she'd no idea where she'd get the money to buy the place. But she'd heard it was going for a song since it was in such bad shape. Her brother Will could do the renovation work and share in the income they'd make from making it a bed and breakfast.

When she finished eating, she strolled around to the front. The "for sale" sign was gone, and a "sold" sign replaced it. Her stomach clenched, and her heart nearly stopped beating. Who would buy that old wreck?

The thought that it would be torn down brought tears to her eyes. No way could she allow that beautiful place to become simply a memory. She had walked for hours, trying to come up with a plan to save the old house. If she couldn't live there, couldn't work there, she could at least make sure no one took it down.

Thursday evening, she showed up at the town council meeting. When the question of who would chair the landmark committee came up, Jess raised her hand.

"I volunteer."

Rick Winslow, chair of the council, recognized her.

"Okay, Jess. You've got it. Any proposals?"

"Yes, I propose that the old Hadley house on Route 32 be considered a landmark."

"That old eyesore?" Rick cringed.

"That house was built in 1795. It's got tons of history. We have to protect it. Keep it from being torn down."

"Okay. You feel so strongly about it. I don't see a problem. Let's take a vote."

The measure passed. Although Jess's heart was heavy, satisfaction at having saved the house warmed her. If she couldn't have it, at least it wouldn't be demolished. She didn't care if the new owner liked that idea or not.

IN HIS PENTHOUSE APARTMENT on Central Park West, Case Hadley, CEO of Hadley Investments, picked up the phone.

"What is it, Charles?"

Charles Hanover, Case's right-hand man, didn't often call him during dinner.

"Bad news, sir."

"What is it?" Case pushed away from the table and strode into the living room. He always paced when on the phone, especially when he got bad news.

"We can't go forward with the demolition."

"What demolition?"

"Your aunt's old place? In Pine Grove?"

"That old disaster? Why not?"

"The town has declared it a landmark. Our contractor can't get a demolition permit."

"What?"

"That's right, sir."

"Shit. Of all the stupid ideas. That place is practically falling down. It'd take millions to renovate it."

"I'm sorry, sir."

"Not your fault, Charles. Thank you for calling."

Case hung up the phone and stood by the window. He'd inherited the old place from his dotty old aunt, Martha Hadley. She'd died penniless. He'd been supporting her for the past ten years. And she'd wanted to repay him by leaving him her house.

He had a business to run and no time for silly things like this.

"Martha would be pleased," he said out loud.

She'd invited him to visit often, but he hated the country. The bugs, the animals, the lack of hot water, no delis, no five-star restaurants. Pine Grove was the last place he'd ever live.

"Sorry, Martha. I'll renovate it, sell it, and give the money to your favorite charity."

He returned to the table, finished the bottle of two-hundred-year-old wine, and retired to the den to go over financial statements from companies he planned to buy and break up.

THE END

About the Author

JEAN JOACHIM IS A BEST-selling romance fiction author, with books hitting the Amazon Top 100 list since 2012. She writes contemporary romance, which includes sports romance and romantic suspense.

Dangerous Love Lost & Found, First Place winner in the 2015 Oklahoma Romance Writers of America, International Digital Award contest. *The Renovated Heart* won Best Novel of the Year from Love Romances Café. *Lovers & Liars* was a RomCon finalist in 2013. And *The Marriage List* tied for third place as Best Contemporary Romance from the Gulf Coast RWA.

To Love or Not to Love tied for second place in the 2014 New England Chapter of Romance Writers of America Reader's Choice contest.

She was chosen Author of the Year in 2012 by the New York City chapter of RWA.

Married and the mother of two sons, Jean lives in New York City. Early in the morning, you'll find her at her computer, writing, with a cup of tea, her rescued pug, Homer, by her side and a secret stash of black licorice.